Sarah's mother—or Richard's wife . . .

"Either Sarah gets out of here, or I do."

Sarah turned passionately to Ann, flinging herself down beside her.

"Mother, Mother, you won't turn me out? You won't, will you? You're my mother."

A flush rose in Ann's face. She said with sudden firmness: "I shall not ask my only daughter to leave her home unless she wants to do so."

Richard shouted: "She would want to—if it weren't to spite me."

Ann raised her hands to her head.

"I can't bear this," she said, "I'm warning you both, I can't bear it . . ."

Sarah cried appealingly:

"Mother . . ."

Richard turned on Ann angrily:

"It's no use, Ann. *You've got to choose . . . .*"

"A Christie book sweeps the reader into the net."
—*The New York Times*

Books by Agatha Christie
writing as Mary Westmacott
from Jove

GIANT'S BREAD
UNFINISHED PORTRAIT
ABSENT IN THE SPRING
THE ROSE AND THE YEW TREE
A DAUGHTER'S A DAUGHTER
THE BURDEN

MARY WESTMACOTT

known to millions as

AGATHA CHRISTIE

A DAUGHTER'S
A DAUGHTER

JOVE BOOKS, NEW YORK

A DAUGHTER'S A DAUGHTER

A Jove Book / published by arrangement with
Rosalind Hicks

PRINTING HISTORY
William Heinemann Ltd. edition published 1952
Two previous Dell editions
New Dell edition / May 1982
Jove edition / March 1988

ISBN: 0-515-09494-3

Jove Books are published by The Berkley Publishing Group,
200 Madison Avenue, New York, New York 10016.
The name "JOVE" and the "J" logo
are trademarks belonging to Jove Publications, Inc.

PRINTED IN THE UNITED STATES OF AMERICA

10 9 8 7 6 5 4 3 2

A DAUGHTER'S
A DAUGHTER

BOOK 1

Chapter one

1

Ann Prentice stood on the platform at Victoria, waving.

The boat train drew out in a series of purposeful jerks, Sarah's dark head disappeared, and Ann Prentice turned to walk slowly down the platform towards the exit.

She experienced the strangely mixed sensations that seeing a loved one off may occasionally engender.

Darling Sarah—how she would miss her. . . . Of course it was only for three weeks. . . . But the flat would seem so empty. . . . Just herself and Edith—two dull middle-aged women. . . .

Sarah was so alive, so vital, so positive about everything. . . . And yet still such a darling black-haired baby—

How awful! What a way to think! How frightfully annoyed Sarah would be! The one thing that Sarah—and all the other girls of her age—seemed to insist upon was an attitude of casual indifference on the part of their parents. "No *fuss*, Mother," they said urgently.

They accepted, of course, tribute in kind. Taking their clothes to the cleaners and fetching them and usually paying for them. Difficult telephone calls ("If *you* just ring Carol up, it will be so much *easier*, Mother.") Clearing up the incessant untidiness. ("Darling, I did mean to take away my messes. But I have simply got to *rush*.")

"Now when I was young," reflected Ann. . . .

Her thoughts went back. Hers had been an old-fashioned home. Her mother had been a woman of over forty when she was born, her father older still, fifteen or sixteen years older than her mother. The house had been run in the way her father liked.

Affection had not been taken for granted, it had been expressed on both sides.

"There's my dear little girl." "Father's pet!" "Is there anything I can get you, Mother darling?"

Tidying up the house, odd errands, tradesmen's books, invitations and social notes, all these Ann had attended to as a matter of course. Daughters existed to serve their parents—not the other way about.

As she passed near the bookstall, Ann asked herself suddenly, "Which was the best?"

Surprisingly enough, it didn't seem an easy question to answer.

Running her eyes along the publications on the bookstall (something to read this evening in front of the fire) she came to the unexpected decision that it didn't really matter. The whole thing was a convention, nothing more. Like using slang. At one period one said things were "topping," and then that they were "too divine," and then that they were "marvellous," and that one "couldn't agree with you more," and that you were "madly" fond of this that and the other.

Children waited on parents, or parents waited on children —it made no difference to the underlying vital relationship of person to person. Between Sarah and herself there was, Ann believed, a deep and genuine love. Between her and her own mother? Looking back she thought that under the surface fondness and affection there had been, actually, that casual and kindly indifference which it was the fashion to assume nowadays.

Smiling to herself, Ann bought a Penguin, a book that she remembered reading some years ago and enjoying. Perhaps it might seem a little sentimental now, but that wouldn't matter, as Sarah was not going to be there . . .

Ann thought: "I shall miss her—of course I shall miss her —but it will be rather *peaceful*. . . ."

And she thought: "It will be a rest for Edith, too. She gets upset when plans are always being changed and meals altered."

For Sarah and her friends were always in a flux of coming and going and ringing up and changing plans. "Mother darling, can we have a meal early? We want to go to a movie." "Is that you, Mother? I rang up to say I shan't be in to lunch after all."

To Edith, that faithful retainer of over twenty years' service, now doing three times the work she was once expected to undertake, such interruptions to normal life were very irritating.

Edith, in Sarah's phrase, often turned sour.

Not that Sarah couldn't get round Edith any time she liked. Edith might scold and grumble, but she adored Sarah.

It would be very quiet alone with Edith. Peaceful—but very quiet. . . . A queer cold feeling made Ann give a little shiver. . . . She thought: "Nothing but quietness now —" Quietness stretching forward vaguely down the slopes of old age into death. Nothing, any more, to look forward to.

"But what do I want?" she asked herself. "I've had everything. Love and happiness with Patrick. A child. I've had all I wanted from life. Now—it's over. Now Sarah will go on where I leave off. She will marry, have children. I shall be a grandmother."

She smiled to herself. She would enjoy being a grandmother. She pictured handsome spirited children, Sarah's children. Naughty little boys with Sarah's unruly black hair, plump little girls. She would read to them—tell them stories . . .

She smiled at the prospect—but the cold feeling was still there. If only Patrick had lived. The old rebellious sorrow rose up. It was so long ago now—when Sarah was only three—so long ago that the loss and the agony were healed. She could think of Patrick gently, without a pang. The impetuous young husband that she had loved so much. So far away now—far away in the past.

But today rebellion rose up anew. If Patrick was still alive, Sarah would go from them—to Switzerland for winter sports, to a husband and a home in due course—and she and Patrick would be there together, older, quieter, but sharing life and its ups and downs together. She would not be alone . . .

Ann Prentice came out into the crowded life of the station yard. She thought to herself: "How sinister all those red buses look—drawn up in line like monsters waiting to be fed." They seemed fantastically to have a sentient life of their own—a life that was, perhaps, inimical to their maker, Man.

What a busy, noisy, crowded world it was, everyone coming and going, hurrying, rushing, talking, laughing, complaining, full of greetings and partings.

And suddenly, once again, she felt that cold pang—of aloneness.

She thought: "It's time Sarah went away—I'm getting too dependent on her. I'm making her, perhaps, too dependent on *me*. I mustn't do that. One mustn't hold on to the young —stop them leading their own lives. That would be wicked —really wicked . . ."

She must efface herself, keep well in the background, encourage Sarah to make her own plans—her own friends.

And then she smiled, because there was really no need to encourage Sarah at all. Sarah had quantities of friends and was always making plans, rushing about here and there with the utmost confidence and enjoyment. She adored her mother, but treated her with a kindly patronage, as one excluded from all understanding and participation, owing to her advanced years.

How old to Sarah seemed the age of forty-one—whilst to Ann it was quite a struggle to call herself in her own mind middle aged. Not that she attempted to keep time at bay. She used hardly any make-up, and her clothes still had the faintly countrified air of a young matron come to town—neat coats and skirts and a small string of real pearls.

Ann sighed. "I can't think why I'm so silly," she said to herself aloud. "I suppose it's just seeing Sarah off."

What did the French say? *Partir, c'est mourrir un peu.* . . .

Yes, that was true. . . . Sarah, swept away by that important puffing train, was, for the moment, dead to her mother. And "I to her," thought Ann. "A curious thing—distance. Separation in space. . . ."

Sarah, living one life. She, Ann, living another. . . . A life of her own.

Some faintly pleasurable sensation replaced the inner chill of which she had previously been conscious. She could choose now when she would get up, what she should do—she could plan her day. She could go to bed early with a meal on a tray—or go out to a theatre or a cinema. Or she could take a train into the country and wander about . . . walking through bare woods with the blue sky showing between the intricate sharp pattern of the branches. . . .

Of course, actually she could do all these things at any time she liked. But when two people lived together, there was a tendency for one life to set the pattern. Ann had enjoyed a good deal, at second hand, Sarah's vivid comings and goings.

No doubt about it, it was great fun being a mother. It was like having your own life over again—with a great deal of the agonies of youth left out. Since you knew now how little some things mattered, you could smile indulgently over the crises that arose.

"But really, Mother," Sarah would say intensely, "it's frightfully serious. You mustn't smile. Nadia feels that the whole of her future is at stake!"

But at forty-one, one had learned that one's whole future was very seldom at stake. Life was far more elastic and resilient than one had once chosen to think.

During her service with an ambulance during the war, Ann had realised for the first time how much the small things of life mattered. The small envies and jealousies, the small pleasures, the chafing of a collar, a chilblain inside a tight shoe—all these ranked as far more immediately important than the great fact that you might be killed at any moment. That should have been a solemn, an overwhelming thought, but actually one became used to it very quickly—and the small things asserted their sway—perhaps heightened in their insistence just because, in the background, was the idea of there being very little time. She had learnt something, too, of the curious inconsistencies of human nature, of how difficult it was to assess people as "good" or "bad" as she had been inclined to do in her days of youthful dogmatism. She had seen unbelievable courage spent in rescuing a victim—and then that same individual who had risked his life would stoop to some mean petty theft from the rescued individual he had just saved.

People, in fact, were not all of a piece.

Standing irresolutely on the kerb, the sharp hooting of a taxi recalled Ann from abstract speculations to more practical considerations. What should she do now, at this moment?

Getting Sarah off to Switzerland had been so far as her mind had looked that morning. That evening she was going out to dine with James Grant. Dear James, always so kind and thoughtful. "You'll feel a bit flat with Sarah gone. Come out and have a little celebration." Really, it was very sweet of James. All very well for Sarah to laugh and call James "Your *pukka Sahib* boy friend, darling." James was a very dear person. Sometimes it might be a little difficult to keep one's attention fixed when he was telling one of his very long and rambling stories, but he enjoyed telling them so much, and after all if one had known someone for twenty-five years, to listen kindly was the least one could do.

Ann glanced at her watch. She might go to the Army and Navy Stores. There were some kitchen things Edith had been wanting. This decision solved her immediate problem. But all the time that she was examining saucepans and asking prices (really fantastic now!) she was conscious of that queer cold panic at the back of her mind.

Finally, on an impulse, she went into a telephone box and dialled a number.

"Can I speak to Dame Laura Whitstable, please?"

"Who is speaking?"

"Mrs. Prentice."

"Just a moment, Mrs. Prentice."

There was a pause and then a deep resonant voice said: "Ann?"

"Oh, Laura, I knew I oughtn't to ring you up at this time of day, but I've just seen Sarah off, and I wondered if you were terribly busy today——"

The voice said with decision:

"Better lunch with me. Rye bread and buttermilk. That suit you?"

"Anything will suit me. It's angelic of you."

"Be expecting you. Quarter-past one."

2

It was one minute to the quarter-past when Ann paid off her taxi in Harley Street and rang the bell.

The competent Harkness opened the door, smiled a welcome, said: "Go straight on up, will you, Mrs. Prentice? Dame Laura may be a few minutes still."

Ann ran lightly up the stairs. The dining-room of the house was now a waiting-room and the top floor of the tall house was converted into a comfortable flat. In the sitting-room a small table was laid for a meal. The room itself was more like a man's room than a woman's. Large sagging comfortable chairs, a wealth of books, some of them piled on the chairs, and rich-coloured good quality velvet curtains.

Ann had not long to wait. Dame Laura, her voice preceding her up the stairs like a triumphant bassoon, entered the room and kissed her guest affectionately.

Dame Laura Whitstable was a woman of sixty-four. She carried with her the atmosphere that is exuded by royalty, or well-known public characters. Everything about her was a little more than life size, her voice, her uncompromising shelf-like bust, the piled masses of her iron-grey hair, her beak-like nose.

"Delighted to see you, my dear child," she boomed. "You look very pretty, Ann. I see you've bought yourself a bunch of violets. Very discerning of you. It's the flower you most resemble."

"The shrinking violet? Really, Laura."

"Autumn sweetness, well concealed by leaves."

"This is most unlike you, Laura. You are usually so rude!"

"I find it pays, but it's rather an effort sometimes. Let us eat immediately. Bassett, where is Bassett? Ah, there you are. There is a sole for you, Ann, you will be glad to hear. And a glass of hock."

"Oh, Laura, you shouldn't. Buttermilk and rye bread would have done quite well."

"There's only just enough buttermilk for me. Come on, sit down. So Sarah's gone off to Switzerland? For how long?"

"Three weeks."

"Very nice."

The angular Bassett had left the room. Sipping her glass of buttermilk with every appearance of enjoyment, Dame Laura said shrewdly:

"And you're going to miss her. But you didn't ring me up and come here to tell me that. Come on, now, Ann. Tell me. We haven't got much time. I know you're fond of me, but when people ring up, and want my company at a moment's notice, it's usually my superior wisdom that's the attraction."

"I feel horribly guilty," said Ann apologetically.

"Nonsense, my dear. Actually, it's rather a compliment."

Ann said with a rush:

"Oh, Laura, I'm a complete fool, I know! But I got in a sort of *panic*. There in Victoria Station with all the buses! I felt—I felt so terribly *alone*."

"Ye-es, I see . . ."

"It wasn't just Sarah going away and missing her. It was more than that . . ."

Laura Whitstable nodded, her shrewd grey eyes watching Ann dispassionately.

Ann said slowly:

"Because, after all, one is always alone . . . really—"

"Ah, so you've found that out? One does, of course, sooner or later. Curiously enough, it's usually a shock. How old are you, Ann? Forty-one? A very good age to make your discovery. Leave it until too late and it can be devastating. Discover it too young—and it takes a lot of courage to acknowledge it."

"Have you ever felt really alone, Laura?" Ann asked with curiosity.

"Oh, yes. It came to me when I was twenty-six—actually in the middle of a family gathering of the most affectionate nature. It startled me and frightened me—but I accepted it. Never deny the truth. One must accept the fact that we have only one companion in this world, a companion who accompanies us from the cradle to the grave—our own self. Get on good terms with that companion—*learn to live with yourself*. That's the answer. It's not always easy."

Ann sighed.

"Life felt absolutely pointless—I'm telling you everything, Laura—just years stretching ahead with nothing to fill them. Oh, I suppose I'm just a silly useless woman . . ."

"Now, now, keep your common sense. You did a very good efficient unspectacular job in the war, you've brought up Sarah to have nice manners and to enjoy life, and in your quiet way you enjoy life yourself. That's all very satisfactory. In fact, if you came to my consulting room I'd send you away without even collecting a fee—and I'm a money-grubbing old woman."

"Laura dear, you are very comforting. But I suppose, really—I do care for Sarah too much."

"Fiddle!"

"I am always so afraid of becoming one of those possessive mothers who positively eat their young."

Laura Whitstable said dryly:

"There's so much talk about possessive mothers that some women are afraid to show a normal affection for their young!"

"But possessiveness *is* a bad thing!"

"Of course it is. I come across it every day. Mothers who keep their sons tied to their apron strings, fathers who monopolise their daughters. But it's not always entirely their doing. I had a nest of birds in my room once, Ann. In due course the fledglings left the nest, but there was one who wouldn't go. Wanted to stay in the nest, wanted to be fed, refused to face the ordeal of tumbling over the edge. It disturbed the mother bird very much. She showed him, flew down again and again from the edge of the nest, chirruped to him, fluttered her wings. Finally she wouldn't feed him. Brought food in her beak, but stayed the other side of the room calling him. Well, there are human beings like that. Children who don't want to grow up, who don't want to face the difficulties of adult life. It isn't their upbringing. It's *themselves*."

She paused before going on.

"There's the wish to be possessed as well as the wish to possess. Is it a case of maturing late? Or is it some inherent lack of the adult quality? One knows very little still of the human personality."

"Anyway," said Ann, uninterested in generalities, "you don't think I'm a possessive mother?"

"I've always thought that you and Sarah had a very satisfactory relationship. I should say there was a deep natural love between you." She added thoughtfully: "Of course Sarah's young for her age."

"I've always thought she was old for her age."

"I shouldn't say so. She strikes me as younger than nineteen in mentality."

"But she's very positive, very assured. And quite sophisticated. Full of her own ideas."

"Full of the current ideas, you mean. It will be a very long time before she has any ideas that are *really* her own. And all these young creatures nowadays seem positive. They need reassurance, that's why. We live in an uncertain age and everything is unstable and the young feel it. That's where half the trouble starts nowadays. Lack of stability. Broken homes. Lack of moral standards. A young plant, you know, needs tying up to a good firm stake."

She grinned suddenly.

"Like all old women, even if I am a distinguished one, I preach." She drained her glass of buttermilk. "Do you know why I drink this?"

"Because it's healthy?"

"Bah! I like it. Always have since I went for holidays to a farm in the country. The other reason is so as to be different.

One poses. We all pose. Have to. I do it more than most. But, thank God, I know I'm doing it. But now about you, Ann. There's nothing wrong with you. You're just getting your second wind, that's all."

"What do you mean by my second wind, Laura? You don't mean—" she hesitated.

"I don't mean anything physical. I'm talking in mental terms. Women are lucky, although ninety-nine out of a hundred don't know it. At what age did St. Theresa set out to reform the monasteries? At fifty. And I could quote you a score of other cases. From twenty to forty women are biologically absorbed—and rightly so. Their concern is with children, with husbands, with lovers—with personal relations. Or they sublimate these things and fling themselves into a career in a female emotional way. But the natural second blooming is of the mind and spirit and it takes place at middle age. Women take more interest in impersonal things as they grow older. Men's interests grow narrower, women's grow wider. A man of sixty is usually repeating himself like a gramophone record. A woman of sixty, if she's got any individuality at all—is an interesting person."

Ann thought of James Grant and smiled.

"Women stretch out to something new. Oh, they make fools of themselves too at that age. Sometimes they're sex bound. But middle age is an age of great possibilities."

"How comforting you are, Laura! Do you think I ought to take up something? Social work of some kind?"

"How much do you love your fellow beings?" said Laura Whitstable gravely. "The deed is no good without the inner fire. Don't do things you don't want to do, and then pat yourself on the back for doing them! Nothing, if I may say so, produces a more odious result. If you enjoy visiting the sick old women, or taking unattractive mannerless brats to the seaside by all means do it. Quite a lot of people do enjoy it. No, Ann, don't force yourself into activities. Remember all ground has sometimes to lie fallow. Motherhood has been your crop up to now. I don't see you becoming a reformer, or an artist, or an exponent of the Social Services. You're quite an ordinary woman, Ann, but a very nice one. Wait. Just wait quietly, with faith and hope, and you'll see. Something worth while will come to fill your life."

She hesitated and then said:

"You've never had an affair, have you?"

Ann flushed.

"No." She braced herself. "Do you—do you think I ought to?"

Dame Laura gave a terrific snort, a vast explosive sound that shook the glasses on the table.

"All this modern cant! In Victorian days we were afraid of sex, draped the legs of the furniture, even! Hid sex away, shoved it out of sight. All very bad. But nowadays we've gone to the opposite extreme. We treat sex like something you order from the chemist. It's on a par with sulphur drugs and penicillin. Young women come and ask me, 'Had I better take a lover?' 'Do you think I ought to have a child?' You'd think it was a sacred duty to go to bed with a man instead of a pleasure. You're not a passionate woman, Ann. You're a woman with a very deep store of affection and tenderness. That can include sex, but sex doesn't come first with you. If you ask me to prophesy, I'll say that in due course you'll marry again."

"Oh no. I don't believe I could ever do that."

"Why did you buy a bunch of violets today and pin them in your coat? You buy flowers for your rooms but you don't usually wear them. Those violets are a symbol, Ann. You bought them because, deep down, you feel spring—your second spring is near."

"St. Martin's summer, you mean," said Ann ruefully.

"Yes, if you like to call it that."

"But really, Laura, I daresay it's a very pretty idea, but I only bought these violets because the woman who was selling them looked so cold and miserable."

"That's what *you* think. But that's only the superficial reason. Look down to the real motive, Ann. Learn to *know* yourself. That's the most important thing in life—to try and know yourself. Heavens—it's past two. I must fly. What are you doing this evening?"

"I'm going out to dinner with James Grant."

"Colonel Grant? Yes, of course. A nice fellow." Her eyes twinkled. "He's been after you for a long time, Ann."

Ann Prentice laughed and blushed.

"Oh, it's just a habit."

"He's asked you to marry him several times, hasn't he?"

"Yes, but it's all nonsense really. Oh, Laura, do you think —perhaps—I ought to? If we're both lonely—"

"There's no *ought* about marriage, Ann! And the wrong companion is worse than none. Poor Colonel Grant—not that I pity him really. A man who continually asks a woman to marry him and can't make her change her mind, is a man who secretly enjoys devotion to lost causes. If he was at Dunkirk, he would have enjoyed it—but I daresay the Charge of the Light Brigade would have suited him far better! How fond we are in this country of our defeats and our blunders—and how ashamed we always seem to be of our victories!"

Chapter two

1

Ann arrived back at her flat to be greeted by the faithful Edith in a somewhat cold fashion.

"A nice bit of plaice I had for your lunch," she said, appearing at the kitchen door. "*And* a caramel custard."

"I'm so sorry. I had lunch with Dame Laura. I did telephone you in time that I shouldn't be in, didn't I?"

"I hadn't cooked the plaice," admitted Edith grudgingly. She was a tall lean women with the upright carriage of a grenadier and a pursed-up disapproving mouth.

"It's not like you, though, to go chopping and changing. With Miss Sarah, now, I shouldn't have been surprised. I found those fancy gloves she was looking for after she'd gone and it was too late. Stuffed down behind the sofa they were."

"What a pity." Ann took the gaily knitted woollen gloves. "She got off all right."

"And happy to go, I suppose."

"Yes, the whole party was very gay."

"Mayn't come back quite so gay. Back on crutches as likely as not."

"Oh no, Edith, don't say that."

"Dangerous, these Swiss places. Fracture your arms or your legs and then not set proper. Goes to gangrene under the plaster and that's the end of you. Awful smell, too."

"Well, we'll hope that won't happen to Sarah," said Ann, well used to Edith's gloomy pronouncements which were always uttered with considerable relish.

"Won't seem like the same place without Miss Sarah about," said Edith. "We shan't know ourselves, we'll be so quiet."

"It will give you a bit of a rest, Edith."

"Rest?" said Edith indignantly. "What would I want with a rest? Better wear out than rust out, that's what my mother used to say to me, and it's what I've always gone by. Now Miss Sarah's away and she and her friends won't be popping in and out every minute I can get down to a real good clean. This place needs it."

"I'm sure the flat's beautifully clean, Edith."

"That's what you think. But I know better. All the curtains want to be took down and well shook, and them lustres on the electrics could do with a wash—oh! there's a hundred and one things need doing."

Edith's eyes gleamed with pleasurable anticipation.

"Get someone in to help you."

"What, me? No fear. I like things done the proper way, and it's not many of these women you can trust to do that nowadays. You've got nice things here and nice things should be kept nice. What with cooking and one thing and another I can't get down to my proper work as I should."

"But you do cook beautifully, Edith. You know you do."

A faintly gratified smile transformed Edith's habitual expression of profound disapproval.

"Oh, cooking," she said in an off-hand way. "There's nothing to *that*. It's not what I call proper work, not by a long way."

Moving back into the kitchen, she asked:

"What time will you have your tea?"

"Oh, not just yet. About half-past four."

"If I were you I'd put your feet up and take a nap. Then you'll be fresh for this evening. Might as well enjoy a bit of peace while you've got it."

Ann laughed. She went into the sitting-room and let Edith settle her comfortably on the sofa.

"You look after me as though I were a little girl, Edith."

"Well, you weren't much more when I first came to your ma, and you haven't changed much. Colonel Grant rang up. Said not to forget it was the Mogador Restaurant at eight o'clock. She knows, I said to him. But that's men all over—fuss, fuss, fuss, and military gentlemen are the worst."

"It's nice of him to think I might be lonely tonight and ask me out."

Edith said judicially:

"I've nothing against the colonel. Fussy he may be, but he's the right kind of gentleman." She paused and added: "On the whole you might do a lot worse than Colonel Grant."

"What did you say, Edith?"

Edith returned an unblinking stare.

"I said as there were worse gentlemen . . . Oh well, I suppose we shan't be seeing so much of that Mr. Gerry now Miss Sarah's gone away."

"You don't like him, do you, Edith?"

"Well, I do and I don't, if you know what I mean. He's got a way with him—that you can't deny. But he's not the steady sort. My sister's Marlene married one like that. Never in a job more than six months, he isn't. And whatever happens it's never his fault."

Edith went out of the room and Ann leaned her head back against the cushions and shut her eyes.

The sound of the traffic came faint and muted through the closed window, a pleasant humming sound like far-off bees. On the table near her a bowl of yellow jonquils sent their sweetness into the air.

She felt peaceful and happy. She was going to miss Sarah, but it was rather restful to be by herself for a short time.

What a queer panic she had had this morning . . .

She wondered what James Grant's party would consist o
this evening.

2

The Mogador was a small rather old-fashioned restaurant
with good food and wine and an unhurried air about it

Ann was the first of the party to arrive and found Colonel
Grant sitting in the reception bar opening and shutting his
watch.

"Ah, Ann," he sprang up to greet her. "Here you are.
His eyes went with approval over her black dinner dress and
the single string of pearls round her throat. "It's a great thing
when a pretty woman can be punctual."

"I'm three minutes late, no more," said Ann, smiling up
at him.

James Grant was a tall man with a stiff soldierly bearing
close-cropped grey hair and an obstinate chin.

He consulted his watch again.

"Now why can't these other people turn up? Our table will
be ready for us at a quarter-past eight and we want some
drinks first. Sherry for you? You prefer it to a cocktail
don't you?"

"Yes, please. Who are the others?"

"The Massinghams. You know them?"

"Of course."

"And Jennifer Graham. She's a first cousin of mine, but
I don't know whether you ever——"

"I met her once with you, I think."

"And the other man is Richard Cauldfield. I only ran into
him the other day. Hadn't seen him for years. He's spent
most of his life in Burma. Feels a bit out of things coming
back to this country."

"Yes, I suppose so."

"Nice fellow. Rather a sad story. Wife died having her
first child. He was devoted to her. Couldn't get over it for a
long time. Felt he had to get right away—that's why he went
out to Burma."

"And the baby?"

"Oh, that died, too."

"How sad."

"Ah, here come the Massinghams."

Mrs. Massingham, always alluded to by Sarah as "the Mem Sahib" bore down upon them in a grand flashing of teeth. She was a lean stringy woman, her skin bleached and dried by years in India. Her husband was a short tubby man with a staccato style of conversation.

"How nice to see you again," said Mrs. Massingham, shaking Ann warmly by the hand. "And how delightful to be coming out to dinner properly dressed. Positively I never seem to wear an evening dress. Everyone always says, 'Don't change.' I do think life is drab nowadays, and the things one has to do oneself! I seem to be always at the sink! I really don't think we can stay in this country. We've been considering Kenya."

"Lot of people clearing out," said her husband. "Fed up. Blinking government."

"Ah, here's Jennifer," said Colonel Grant, "and Cauldfield."

Jennifer Graham was a tall horse-faced woman of thirty-five who whinnied when she laughed. Richard Cauldfield was a middle-aged man with a sunburned face.

He sat down by Ann and she began to make conversation. Had he been in England long? What did he think of things?

It took a bit of getting used to, he said. Everything was so different from what it was before the war. He'd been looking for a job—but jobs weren't so easy to find, not for a man of his age.

"No, I believe that's true. It seems all wrong somehow."

"Yes, after all I'm still the right side of fifty." He smiled a rather child-like and disarming smile. "I've got a small amount of capital. I'm wondering about buying a small place in the country. Going in for market gardening. Or chickens."

"*Not* chickens!" said Ann. "I've several friends who have tried chickens—and they always seem to get diseases."

"No, perhaps market gardening would be better. One wouldn't make much of a profit, perhaps, but it would be a pleasant life."

He sighed.

"Things are so much in the melting-pot. Perhaps if we get a change of government—"

Ann acquiesced doubtfully. It was the usual panacea.

"It must be difficult to know what exactly to go in for," she said. "Quite worrying."

"Oh, I don't worry. I don't believe in worry. If a man has faith in himself and proper determination, every difficulty will straighten itself out."

It was a dogmatic assertion and Ann looked doubtful.

"I wonder," she said.

"I can assure you that it is so. I've no patience with people who go about always whining about their bad luck."

"Oh, there I do agree," exclaimed Ann with such fervour that he raised his eyebrows questioningly.

"You sound as though you had experience of something of the kind."

"I have. One of my daughter's boy friends is always coming and telling us of his latest misfortune. I used to be sympathetic, but now I've become both callous and bored."

Mrs. Massingham said across the table:

"Hard-luck stories *are* boring."

Colonel Grant said:

"Who are you talking of, young Gerald Lloyd? He'll never amount to much."

Richard Cauldfield said quietly to Ann:

"So you have a daughter? And a daughter old enough to have a boy friend."

"Oh yes. Sarah is nineteen."

"And you're very fond of her?"

"Of course."

She saw a momentary expression of pain across his face and remembered the story Colonel Grant had told her.

Richard Cauldfield was, she thought, a lonely man.

He said in a low voice:

"You look too young to have a grown-up daughter. . . ."

"That's the regulation thing to say to a woman of my age," said Ann with a laugh.

"Perhaps. But I meant it. Your husband is—" he hesitated —"dead?"

"Yes, a long time ago."

"Why haven't you remarried?"

It might have been an impertinent question, but the real interest in his voice saved it from any false imputation of that kind. Again Ann felt that Richard Cauldfield was a simple person. He really wanted to know.

"Oh, because—" she stopped. Then she spoke truthfully and with sincerity. "I loved my husband very much. After he died I never fell in love with anyone else. And there was Sarah, of course."

"Yes," said Cauldfield. "Yes—with you that is exactly what it would be."

Grant got up and suggested that they move into the restaurant. At the round table Ann sat next to her host with Major Massingham on her other side. She had no further opportunity of a *tête-à-tête* with Cauldfield, who was talking rather ponderously with Miss Graham.

"Think they might do for each other, eh?" murmured the colonel in her ear. "He needs a wife, you know."

For some reason the suggestion displeased Ann. Jennifer Graham, indeed, with her loud hearty voice and her neighing laugh! Not at all the sort of woman for a man like Cauldfield to marry.

Oysters were brought and the party settled down to food and talk.

"Sarah gone off this morning?"

"Yes, James. I do hope they'll have some good snow."

"Yes, it's a bit doubtful this time of year. Anyway, I expect she'll enjoy herself all right. Handsome girl, Sarah. By the way, hope young Lloyd isn't one of the party?"

"Oh no, he's just gone into his uncle's firm. He can't go away."

"Good thing. You must nip all that in the bud, Ann."

"One can't do much nipping in these days, James."

"Hm, suppose not. Still, you've got her away for a while."

"Yes. I thought it would be a good plan."

"Oh, you did? You're no fool, Ann. Let's hope she takes up with some other young fellow out there."

"Sarah's very young still, James. I don't think the Gerry Lloyd business was serious at all."

"Perhaps not. But she seemed very concerned about him when last I saw her."

"Being concerned is rather a thing of Sarah's. She knows exactly what everyone ought to do and makes them do it. She's very loyal to her friends."

"She's a dear child. And a very attractive one. But she'll never be as attractive as you, Ann, she's a harder type—what do they call it nowadays—hard-boiled."

Ann smiled.

"I don't think Sarah's very hard-boiled. It's just the manner of her generation."

"Perhaps so. . . . But some of these girls could take a lesson in charm from their mothers."

He was looking at her affectionately and Ann thought to herself with a sudden unusual warmth: "Dear James. How sweet he is to me. He really does think me perfect. Am I a fool not to accept what he offers? To be loved and cherished—"

Unfortunately at that moment Colonel Grant started telling her the story of one of his subalterns and a major's wife in India. It was a long story and she had heard it three times before.

The affectionate warmth died down. Across the table she watched Richard Cauldfield, appraising him. A little too confident of himself, too dogmatic—no, she corrected herself, not really. . . . That was only a defensive armour he put up against a strange and possibly hostile world.

It was a sad face, really. A lonely face . . .

He had a lot of good qualities, she thought. He would be kind and honest and strictly fair. Obstinate, probably, and occasionally prejudiced. A man unused to laughing at things or being laughed at. The kind of man who would blossom out if he felt himself truly loved—

"—and would you believe it?" the colonel came to a triumphant end to his story "—the Sayce had known about it all the time!"

With a shock Ann came back to her immediate duties and laughed with all the proper appreciation.

Chapter three
1

Ann woke on the following morning and for a moment wondered where she was. Surely, that dim outline of the window should have been on the right, not the left. . . . The door, the wardrobe . . .

Then she realised. She had been dreaming; dreaming that she was back, a girl, in her old home at Applestream. She had come there full of excitement, to be welcomed by her mother, by a younger Edith. She had run round the garden, exclaiming at this and that and had finally entered the house. All was as it had been, the rather dark hall, the chintz-covered drawing-room opening off it. And then, surprisingly, her mother had said: "We're having tea in *here* today," and had led her through a further door into a new and unfamiliar room. An attractive room, with gay chintz covers, and flowers, and sunlight; and someone was saying to her: "*You never knew that these rooms were here, did you? We found them last year!*" There had been more new rooms and a small staircase and more rooms upstairs. It had all been very exciting and thrilling.

Now that she was awake she was still partly in the dream. She was Ann the girl, a creature standing at the beginning of life. Those undiscovered rooms! Fancy never knowing about them all these years! When had they been found? Lately? Or years ago?

Reality seeped slowly through the confused pleasurable dream state. All a dream, a very happy dream. Shot through now with a slight ache, the ache of nostalgia. Because one couldn't go back. And how odd that a dream of discovering additional ordinary rooms in a house should engender such a queer ecstatic pleasure. She felt quite sad to think that these rooms had never actually existed.

Ann lay in bed watching the outline of the window grow clearer. It must be quite late, nine o'clock at least. The mornings were so dark now. Sarah would be waking to sunshine and snow in Switzerland.

But somehow Sarah hardly seemed real at this moment. Sarah was far away, remote, indistinct. . . .

What was real was the house in Cumberland, the chintzes, the sunlight, the flowers—her mother. And Edith, standing respectfully to attention, looking, in spite of her young smooth unlined face, definitely disapproving as usual.

Ann smiled and called: "Edith!"

Edith entered and pulled the curtains back.

"Well," she said approvingly. "You've had a nice lay in. I wasn't going to wake you. It's not much of a day. Fog coming on, I'd say."

The outlook from the window was a heavy yellow. It was not an attractive prospect, but Ann's sense of well-being was not shaken. She lay there smiling to herself.

"Your breakfast's all ready. I'll fetch it in."

Edith paused as she left the room, looking curiously at her mistress.

"Looking pleased with yourself this morning, I must say. You must have enjoyed yourself last night."

"Last night?" Ann was vague for a moment. "Oh, yes, yes. I enjoyed myself very much. Edith, when I woke up I'd been dreaming I was at home again. You were there and it was summer and there were new rooms in the house that we'd never known about."

"Good job we didn't, I'd say," said Edith. "Quite enough rooms as it was. Great rambling old place. And that kitchen! When I think of what that range must have ate in coal! Lucky it was cheap then."

"You were quite young again, Edith, and so was I."

"Ah, we can't put the clock back, can we? Not for all we may want to. Those times are dead and gone for ever."

"Dead and gone for ever," repeated Ann softly.

"Not as I'm not quite satisfied as I am. I've got my health and strength, though they do say it's at middle life you're most liable to get one of these internal growths. I've thought of that once or twice lately."

"I'm sure you haven't got anything of the kind, Edith."

"Ah, but you don't know yourself. Not until the moment when they cart you off to hospital and cuts you up and by then it's usually too late." And Edith left the room with gloomy relish.

She returned a few minutes later with Ann's breakfast tray of coffee and toast.

"There you are, ma'am. Sit up and I'll tuck the pillow behind your back."

Ann looked up at her and said impulsively:

"How good you are to me, Edith."

Edith flushed a fiery red with embarrassment.

"I know the way things should be done, that's all. And anyway, someone's got to look after you. You're not one of these strong-minded ladies. That Dame Laura now—the Pope of Rome himself couldn't stand up to her."

"Dame Laura is a great personality, Edith."

"I know. I've heard her on the radio. Why, just by the look of her you'd always know she was somebody. Managed to get married too, by what I've heard. Was it divorce or death that parted them?"

"Oh, he died."

"Best thing for him, I daresay. She's not the kind any gentleman would find it comfortable to live with—although I won't deny as there's *some* men as actually prefer their wives to wear the trousers."

Edith moved towards the door, observing as she did so:

"Now don't you hurry up, my dear. You just have a nice rest and lay-a-bed and think your pretty thoughts and enjoy your holiday."

"Holiday," thought Ann, amused. "Is that what she calls it?"

And yet in a way it was true enough. It was an interregnum

in the patterned fabric of her life. Living with a child that you loved, there was always a faint clawing anxiety at the back of your mind. "Is she happy?" "Are A. or B. or C. good friends for her?" "Something must have gone wrong at that dance last night. I wonder what it was?"

She had never interfered or asked questions. Sarah, she realised, must feel free to be silent or to talk—must learn her own lessons from life, must choose her own friends. Yet, because you loved her, you could not banish her problems from your mind. And at any moment you might be needed. If Sarah were to turn to her mother for sympathy or for practical help, her mother must be there, ready. . . .

Sometimes Ann had said to herself: "I must be prepared one day to see Sarah unhappy, and even then I must not speak unless she wants me too."

The thing that had worried her lately was that bitter and querulous young man, Gerald Lloyd, and Sarah's increasing absorption in him. That fact lay at the back of her relief that Sarah was separated from him for at least three weeks and would be meeting plenty of other young men.

Yes, with Sarah in Switzerland, she could dismiss her happily from her mind and relax. Relax here in her comfortable bed and think about what she should do today. She'd enjoyed herself very much at the party last night. Dear James—so kind—and yet such a bore, too, poor darling! Those endless stories of his! Really, men, when they got to forty-five, should make a vow not to tell any stories or anecdotes at all. Did they even imagine how their friends' spirits sank when they began: "Don't know whether I ever told you, but rather a curious thing happened once to—" and so on.

One could say, of course: "Yes, James, you've told me three times already." And then the poor darling would look so hurt. No, one couldn't do that to James.

That other man, Richard Cauldfield. He was much younger, of course, but probably *he* would take to repeating long boring stories over and over again one day. . . .

She considered . . . perhaps . . . but she didn't think

so. No, he was more likely to lay down the law, to become didactic. He would have prejudices, preconceived ideas. He would have to be teased, gently teased. . . . He might be a little absurd sometimes, but he was a dear really—a lonely man—a very lonely man. . . . She felt sorry for him. He was so adrift in this modern frustrated life of London. She wondered what sort of job he would get. . . . It wasn't so easy nowadays. He would probably buy his farm or his market garden and settle down in the country.

She wondered whether she would meet him again. She would be asking James to dinner one evening soon. She might suggest he brought Richard Cauldfield with him. It would be a nice thing to do—he was clearly lonely. And she would ask another woman. They might go to a play—

What a noise Edith was making. She was in the sitting-room next door and it sounded as though there were an army of removal men at work. Bangs, bumps, the occasional high whine of the vacuum cleaner. Edith must be enjoying herself.

Presently Edith peeped round the door. Her head was tied up in a duster and she wore the exalted rapt look of a priestess performing a ritual orgy.

"You wouldn't be out to lunch, I suppose? I was wrong about the fog. It's going to be a proper nice day. I don't mean as I've forgotten that bit of plaice. I haven't. But if it's kept till now, it'll keep till this evening. No denying, these fridges do keep things—but it takes the goodness out of them all the same. That's what I say."

Ann looked at Edith and laughed.

"All right, all right, I'll go out to lunch."

"Please yourself, of course. *I* don't mind."

"Yes, Edith, but don't kill yourself. Why not get Mrs. Hopper in to help you, if you must clean the place from top to toe."

"Mrs. Hopper, Mrs. Hopper! I'll Hopper her! I let her clean that nice brass fender of your ma's last time she came. Left it all smeary. Wash down the linoleum, that's all these women are good for, and anybody can do that. Remember that cut-steel fender and grate we had at Applestream? *That* took a bit of keeping. I took a pride in that, I can tell you. Ah well, you've some nice pieces of furniture here and they polish up something beautiful. Pity there's so much built-in stuff."

"It makes less work."

"Too much like a hotel for my liking. So you'll be going out? Good. I can get all the rugs up."

"Can I come here tonight? Or would you like me to go to an hotel?"

"Now then, Miss Ann, none of your jokes. By the way, that double saucepan you brought home from the Stores isn't a mite of good. It's too big for one thing and it's a bad shape for stirring inside. I want one like my old one."

"I'm afraid they don't make them any more, Edith."

"This government," said Edith in disgust. "What about those china soufflé dishes I asked about? Miss Sarah likes a soufflé served that way."

"I forgot you'd asked me to get them. I daresay I could find some of them all right."

"There you are, then. That's something for you to do."

"Really, Edith," cried Ann, exasperated. "I might be a little girl you're telling to go out and have a nice bowl of her hoop."

"Miss Sarah being away makes you seem younger, I must admit. But I was only suggesting, ma'am——" Edith drew herself up to her full height and spoke with sour primness "——if you should happen to be in the neighbourhood of the Army and Navy Stores, or maybe John Barker's——"

"All right, Edith. Go and bowl your own hoop in the sitting-room."

"Well, really," said Edith, outraged, and withdrew.

The bangs and bumps recommenced and presently another sound was added to them, the thin tuneless sound of Edith's voice upraised in a particularly gloomy hymn tune:

"This is a land of pain and woe
No joy, no sun, no light.
Oh lave, Oh lave us in Thy blood
That we may mourn aright."

2

Ann enjoyed herself in the china department of the Army and Navy Stores. She thought that nowadays when so many things were shoddily and badly made, it was a relief to see what good china and glass and pottery this country could turn out still.

The forbidding notices "For Export Only" did not spoil her appreciation of the wares displayed in their shining rows. She passed on to the tables displaying the export rejects where there were always women shoppers hovering with keen glances to pounce on some attractive piece.

Today, Ann herself was fortunate. There was actually a nearly complete breakfast set, with nice wide round cups in an agreeable brown glazed and patterned pottery. The price was not unreasonable and she purchased it just in time. Another woman came along just as the address was being taken and said excitedly: "I'll have that."

"Sorry, madam, I'm afraid it's sold."

Ann said insincerely: "I'm so sorry," and walked away buoyed up with the delight of successful achievement. She had also found some very pleasant soufflé dishes of the right size, but in glass, not china, which she hoped Edith would accept without grumbling too much.

From the china department she went across the street into the gardening department. The window-box outside the flat window was crumbling into disintegration and she wanted to order another.

She was talking to the salesman about it when a voice behind her said:

"Why, good morning, Mrs. Prentice."

She turned to find Richard Cauldfield. His pleasure at their meeting was so evident that Ann could not help feeling flattered.

"Fancy meeting you here like this. It really is a wonderful coincidence. I was just thinking about you as a matter of fact. You know, last night, I wanted to ask you where you lived and if I might, perhaps, come and see you? But then I thought that perhaps you would think it was rather an impertinence on my part. You must have so many friends, and—"

Ann interrupted him.

"Of course you must come and see me. Actually I was thinking of asking Colonel Grant to dinner and suggesting that he might bring you with him."

"Were you? Were you really?"

His eagerness and pleasure were so evident that Ann felt a pang of sympathy. Poor man, he must be lonely. That happy smile of his was really quite boyish.

She said: "I've been ordering myself a new window-box. That's the nearest we can get in a flat to having a garden."

"Yes, I suppose so."

"What are you doing here?"

"I've been looking at incubators—"

"Still hankering after chickens."

"In a way. I've been looking at all the latest poultry equipment. I understand this electrical stunt is the latest thing."

They moved together towards the exit. Richard Cauldfield said in a sudden rush:

"I wonder—of course perhaps you're engaged—whether you'd care to lunch with me—that is if you're not doing anything else."

"Thank you. I'd like to very much. As a matter of fact Edith, my maid, is indulging in an orgy of spring cleaning and has told me very firmly not to come home to lunch."

Richard Cauldfield looked rather shocked and not at all amused.

"That's very arbitrary, isn't it?"

"Edith is privileged."

"All the same, you know, it doesn't do to spoil servants."

He's reproving me, thought Ann with amusement. She said gently:

"There aren't many servants about to spoil. And anyway Edith is more a friend than a servant. She has been with me a great many years."

"Oh, I see." He felt he had been gently rebuked, yet his impression remained. This gentle pretty woman was being bullied by some tyrannical domestic. She wasn't the kind of woman who could stand up for herself. Too sweet and yielding a nature.

He said vaguely: "Spring cleaning? Is this the time of year one does it?"

"Not really. It should be done in March. But my daughter is away for some weeks in Switzerland, so it makes an opportunity. When she's at home there is too much going on."

"You miss her, I expect?"

"Yes, I do."

"Girls don't seem to like staying at home much nowadays. I suppose they're keen on living their own lives."

"Not quite as much as they were, I think. The novelty has rather worn off."

"Oh. It's a very nice day, isn't it? Would you like to walk across the park, or would it tire you?"

"No, of course it wouldn't. I was just going to suggest it to you."

They crossed Victoria Street and went down a narrow passage-way, coming out finally by St. James's Park station. Cauldfield looked up at the Epstein statues.

"Can you see anything whatever in those? How can one call things like that *Art?*"

"Oh, I think one can. Very definitely so."

"Surely you don't *like* them?"

"I don't personally, no. I'm old-fashioned and continue to like classical sculpture and the things I was brought up to like. But that doesn't mean that my taste is right. I think one has to be educated to appreciate new forms of art. The same with music."

"Music! You can't call it music."

"Mr. Cauldfield, don't you think you're being rather narrow-minded?"

He turned his head sharply to look at her. She was flushed, a trifle nervous, but her eyes met his squarely and did not flinch.

"Am I? Perhaps I am. Yes, I suppose when you've been away a long time, you tend to come home and object to everything that isn't strictly as you remember it." He smiled suddenly. "You must take me in hand."

Ann said quickly: "Oh, I'm terribly old-fashioned myself. Sarah often laughs at me. But what I do feel is that it is a terrible pity to—to—how shall I put it?—close one's mind just as one is getting—well, getting old. For one thing, it's going to make one so tiresome—and then, also, one may be missing something that matters."

Richard walked in silence for some moments. Then he said:

"It sounds so absurd to hear you talk of yourself as getting old. You're the youngest person I've met for a long time. Much younger than some of these alarming girls. They really do frighten me."

"Yes, they frighten me a little. But I always find them very kind."

They had reached St. James's Park. The sun was fully out now and the day was almost warm.

"Where shall we go?"

"Let's go and look at the pelicans."

They watched the birds with contentment, and talked about the various species of water fowl. Completely relaxed and at ease, Richard was boyish and natural, a charming companion. They chatted and laughed together and were astonishingly happy in each other's company.

Presently Richard said: "Shall we sit down for a while in the sun? You won't be cold, will you?"

"No, I'm quite warm."

They sat on two chairs and looked out over the water. The scene with its rarefied colouring was like a Japanese print.

Ann said softly: "How beautiful London can be. One doesn't always realise it."

"No. It's almost a revelation."

They sat quietly for a minute or two, then Richard said:

"My wife always used to say that London was the only place to be when spring came. She said the green buds and the almond trees and in time the lilacs all had more significance against a background of bricks and mortar. She said in the country it all happened confusedly and it was too big to see properly. But in a suburban garden spring came overnight."

"I think she was right."

Richard said with an effort, and not looking at Ann:

"She died—a long time ago."

"I know. Colonel Grant told me."

Richard turned and looked at her.

"Did he tell you how she died?"

"Yes."

"That's something I shall never get over. I shall always feel that I killed her."

Ann hesitated a moment, then spoke:

"I can understand what you feel. In your place I should feel as you do. But it isn't true, you know."

"It is true."

"No. Not from her—from a woman's point of view. The responsibility of accepting that risk is the woman's. It's implicit in—in her love. She wants the child, remember. Your wife did—want the child?"

"Oh yes. Aline was very happy about it. So was I. She was a strong healthy girl. There seemed no reason why anything should go wrong."

There was silence again.

Then Ann said: "I'm sorry—so very sorry."

"It's a long time ago now."

"The baby died too?"

"Yes. In a way, you know, I'm glad of that. I should, I feel, have resented the poor little thing. I should always have remembered the price that was paid for its life."

"Tell me about your wife."

Sitting there, in the pale wintry sunlight, he told her about Aline. How pretty she had been and how gay. And the sudden quiet moods she had had when he had wondered what she was thinking about and why she had gone so far away.

Once he broke off to say wonderingly: "I have not spoken about her to anyone for years," and Ann said gently: "Go on."

It had all been so short—too short. A three months' engagement, their marriage—"the usual fuss, we didn't really want it all, but her mother insisted." They had spent their honeymoon motoring in France, seeing the châteaux of the Loire.

He said inconsequentially: "She was nervous in a car, you know. She'd keep her hand on my knee. It seemed to give her confidence, I don't know why she was nervous. She'd never been in an accident." He paused and then went on: "Sometimes, after it had all happened, I used to feel her hand sometimes when I was driving out in Burma. Imagine it, you know. . . . It seemed incredible that she should go right away like that—right out of life. . . ."

Yes, thought Ann, that is what it feels like—incredible. So she had felt about Patrick. He *must* be somewhere. He *must* be able to make her feel his presence. He couldn't go out like that and leave nothing behind. That terrible gulf between the dead and the living!

Richard was going on. Telling her about the little house they had found in a cul-de-sac, with a lilac bush and a pear tree.

Then, when his voice, brusque and hard, came to the end of the halting phrases, he said again wonderingly: "I don't know why I have told you all this. . . ."

But he did know. When he had asked Ann rather nervously if it would be all right to lunch at his club—"they have a kind of Ladies' Annexe, I believe—or would you rather go to a restaurant?"—and when she had said that she would prefer the club, and they had got up and begun to walk towards Pall Mall, the knowledge was in his mind, though not willingly recognised by him.

This was his farewell to Aline, here in the cold unearthly beauty of the park in winter.

He would leave her here, beside the lake, with the bare branches of the trees showing their tracery against the sky.

For the last time, he brought her to life in her youth and her strength and the sadness of her fate. It was a lament, a dirge, a hymn of praise—a little perhaps of all of them.

But it was also a burial.

He left Aline there in the park and walked out into the streets of London with Ann.

Chapter four

"Mrs. Prentice in?" asked Dame Laura Whitstable.

"Not just at present she isn't. But I should fancy she mayn't be long. Would you like to come in and wait, ma'am? I know she'd want to see you."

Edith drew aside respectfully as Dame Laura came in. The latter said:

"I'll wait for a quarter of an hour, anyway. It's some time since I've seen anything of her."

"Yes, ma'am."

Edith ushered her into the sitting-room and knelt down to turn on the electric fire. Dame Laura looked round the room and uttered an exclamation.

"Furniture been shifted round, I see. That desk used to be across the corner. And the sofa's in a different place."

"Mrs. Prentice thought it would be nice to have a change," said Edith. "Come in one day, I did, and there she was shoving things round and hauling them about. 'Oh, Edith,' she says, 'don't you think the room looks much nicer like this? It makes more space.' Well, I couldn't see any improvement myself, but naturally I didn't like to say so. Ladies have their fancies. All I said was: 'Now don't you go and strain yourself, ma'am. Lifting and heaving's the worst thing for your innards and once they've slipped out of place they don't go back so easy.' I should know. It happened to my own sister-in-law. Did it throwing up the window-sash, she did. On the sofa for the rest of her days, she was."

"Probably quite unnecessary," said Dame Laura robustly. "Thank goodness we've got out of the affectation that lying on a sofa is the panacea for every ill."

"Don't even let you have your month after childbirth now," said Edith disapprovingly. "My poor young niece, now, they made her walk about on the fifth day."

"We're a much healthier race now than we've ever been before."

"I hope so, I'm sure," said Edith gloomily. "Terribly delicate I was as a child. Never thought they'd rear me. Fainting fits I used to have, and spasms something awful. And in winter I'd go quite blue—the cold used to fly to me 'art."

Uninterested in Edith's past ailments, Dame Laura was surveying the rearranged room.

"I think it's a change for the better," she said. "Mrs. Prentice is quite right. I wonder she didn't do it before."

"Nest-building," said Edith, with significance.

"What?"

"Nest-building. I've seen birds at it. Running about with twigs in their mouths."

"Oh."

The two women looked at each other. Without any change of expression, some intelligence appeared to be imparted. Dame Laura asked in an off-hand way:

"Seen much of Colonel Grant lately?"

Edith shook her head.

"Poor gentleman," she said. "If you were to ask me, I'd say he's had his conger. French for your nose being put out of joint," she added in an explanatory fashion.

"Oh, *congé*—yes, I see."

"He was a nice gentleman," said Edith, putting him in the past tense in a funereal manner and as though pronouncing an epitaph. "Oh, well!"

As she left the room, she said: "I'll tell you one who won't like the room being rearranged, and that's Miss Sarah. She don't like changes."

Laura Whitstable raised her beetling eyebrows. Then she pulled a book from a shelf and turned its pages in a desultory manner.

Presently she heard a latch-key inserted and the door of the flat opened. Two voices, Ann's and a man's, sounded cheerful and gay in the small vestibule.

Ann's voice said: "Oh, post. Ah, here's a letter from Sarah."

She came into the sitting-room with the letter in her hand and stopped short in momentary confusion.

"Why, Laura, how nice to see you." She turned to the man who had followed her into the room. "Mr. Cauldfield, Dame Laura Whitstable."

Dame Laura summed him up quickly.

Conventional type. Could be obstinate. Honest. Good-hearted. No humour. Probably sensitive. Very much in love with Ann.

She began talking to him in her bluff fashion.

Ann murmured: "I'll tell Edith to bring us tea," and left the room.

"Not for me, my dear," Dame Laura called after her. "It's nearly six o'clock."

"Well, Richard and I want tea, we've been to a concert. What will you have?"

"Brandy and soda."

"All right."

Dame Laura said:

"Fond of music, Mr. Cauldfield?"

"Yes. Particularly of Beethoven."

"All English people like Beethoven. Sends me to sleep, I'm sorry to say, but then I'm not particularly musical."

"Cigarette, Dame Laura?" Cauldfield proffered his case.

"No, thanks, I only smoke cigars."

She added, looking shrewdly at him: "So you're the type of man who prefers tea to cocktails or sherry at six o'clock?"

"No, I don't think so. I'm not particularly fond of tea. But somehow it seems to suit Ann—" he broke off. "That sounds absurd!"

"Not at all. You display perspicacity. I don't mean that Ann doesn't drink cocktails or sherry, she does, but she's essentially the type of woman who looks her best sitting behind a tea-tray—a tea-tray on which is beautiful old Georgian silver and cups and saucers of fine porcelain."

Richard was delighted.

"How absolutely right you are!"

"I've known Ann for a great many years. I'm very fond of her."

"I know. She has often spoken about you. And, of course, I know of you from other sources."

Dame Laura gave him a cheerful grin.

"Oh yes, I'm one of the best-known women in England. Always sitting on committees, or airing my views on the wireless, or laying down the law generally on what's good for humanity. However, I do realize one thing and that is that whatever one accomplishes in life, it is really very little and could always quite easily have been accomplished by somebody else."

"Oh, come now," Richard protested. "Surely that's a very depressing conclusion to come to?"

"It shouldn't be. Humility should always lie behind effort."

"I don't think I agree with you."

"Don't you?"

"No. I think that if a man (or woman, of course) is ever to accomplish anything worth doing, the first condition is that he must believe in himself."

"Why should he?"

"Come now, Dame Laura, surely——"

"I'm old-fashioned. I would prefer that a man should have *knowledge* of himself and *belief* in God."

"Knowledge—belief, aren't they the same thing?"

"I beg your pardon, they're not at all the same thing. One of my pet theories (quite unrealisable, of course, that's the pleasant part about theories) is that everybody should spend one month a year in the middle of a desert. Camped by a well, of course, and plentifully supplied with dates or whatever you eat in deserts."

"Might be quite pleasant," said Richard, smiling. "I'd stipulate for a few of the world's best books, though."

"Ah, but that's just it. No books. Books are a habit-forming drug. With enough to eat and drink, and nothing—absolutely *nothing*—to do, you'd have, at last, a fairly good chance to make acquaintance with yourself."

Richard smiled disbelievingly.

"Don't you think most of us know ourselves pretty well?"

"I certainly do *not*. One hasn't time, in these days, to recognize anything except one's more pleasing characteristics."

"Now what are you two arguing about?" asked Ann coming in with a glass in her hand. "Here's your brandy and soda, Laura. Edith's just bringing tea."

"I'm propounding my desert meditation theory," said Laura.

"That's one of Laura's things," said Ann laughing. "You sit in a desert and do nothing and find out how horrible you really are!"

"Must everyone be horrible?" asked Richard dryly. "I know psychologists tell one so—but really—why?"

"Because if one only has time to know part of oneself one will, as I said just now, select the pleasantest part," said Dame Laura promptly.

"It's all very well, Laura," said Ann, "but after one has sat in one's desert and found out how horrible one is, what good will it do? Will one be able to change oneself?"

"I should think that would be most unlikely—but it does at least give one a guide as to what one is likely to do in certain circumstances, and even more important, *why* one does it?"

"But isn't one able to imagine quite well what one is likely to do in given circumstances? I mean, you've only got to imagine yourself there?"

"Oh Ann, Ann! Think of any man who rehearses in his own mind what he is going to say to his boss, to his girl, to his neighbour across the way. He's got it all cut and dried— and then, when the moment comes, he is either tongue-tied or says something entirely different! The people who are secretly quite sure they can rise to any emergency are the ones who lose their heads completely, while those who are afraid they will be inadequate surprise themselves by taking complete grasp of a situation."

"Yes, but that's not quite fair. What you're meaning now is that people rehearse imaginary conversations and actions *as they would like them to be.* They probably know quite well it wouldn't really happen. But I think fundamentally one *does* know quite well what one's reactions are and what —well, what one's character is like."

"Oh, my dear child." Dame Laura held up her hands. "So

you think you know Ann Prentice—I wonder."

Edith came in with the tea.

"I don't think I'm particularly nice," said Ann smiling.

"Here's Miss Sarah's letter, ma'am," said Edith. "You left it in your bedroom."

"Oh, thank you, Edith."

Ann laid down the still unopened letter by her plate. Dame Laura flashed a quick look at her.

Richard Cauldfield drank his cup of tea rather quickly and then excused himself.

"He's being tactful," said Ann. "He thinks we want to talk together."

Dame Laura looked at her friend attentively. She was quite surprised at the change in Ann. Ann's quiet good looks had bloomed into a kind of beauty. Laura Whitstable had seen that happen before, and she knew the cause. That radiance, that happy look, could have only one meaning: Ann was in love. How unfair it was, reflected Dame Laura, that women in love looked their best and men in love looked like depressed sheep.

"What have you been doing with yourself lately, Ann?" she asked.

"Oh, I don't know. Going about. Nothing much."

"Richard Cauldfield is a new friend, isn't he?"

"Yes. I've only known him about ten days. I met him at James Grant's dinner."

She told Dame Laura something about Richard, ending up by asking naïvely, "You do like him, don't you?"

Laura, who had not yet made up her mind whether she liked Richard Cauldfield or not, was prompt to reply:

"Yes, very much."

"I do feel, you know, that he's had a sad life."

Dame Laura had heard the statement made very often. She suppressed a smile and asked: "What news of Sarah?"

Ann's face lit up.

"Oh, Sarah's been enjoying herself madly. They've had perfect snow, and nobody seems to have broken anything."

Dame Laura said dryly that Edith would be disappointed. They both laughed.

"This letter is from Sarah. Do you mind if I open it?"

"Of course not."

Ann tore open the envelope and read the short letter. Then laughed affectionately and passed the letter to Dame Laura.

Darling Mother, (Sarah had written.)

Snow's been perfect. Everyone's saying it's been the best season ever. Lou took her test but didn't pass unfortunately. Roger's been coaching me a lot—terribly nice of him because he's such a big pot in the ski-ing world. Jane says he's got a thing about me, but I don't really think so. I think it's sadistic pleasure at seeing me tie myself into knots and land on my head in snow-drifts. Lady Cronsham's here with that awful S. American man. They really are *blatant*. I've got rather a crush on one of the guides—unbelievably handsome—but unfortunately he's used to everyone having crushes on him and I cut no ice at all. At last I've learned to waltz on the ice.

How are you getting on, darling? I hope you're going out a good deal with all the boy friends. Don't go too far with the old colonel, he has quite a gay Poona sparkle in his eye sometimes! How's the professor? Has he been telling you any nice rude marriage customs lately? See you soon, Love, Sarah.

Dame Laura handed back the letter.

"Yes, Sarah seems to be enjoying herself. . . . I suppose the professor is that archaeological friend of yours?"

"Yes, Sarah always teases me about him. I really meant to ask him to lunch, but I've been so busy."

"Yes, you do seem to have been busy."

Ann was folding and refolding Sarah's letter. She said with a half sigh: "Oh dear."

"Why the Oh dear, Ann?"

"Oh, I suppose I might as well tell you. Anyway you've probably guessed. Richard Cauldfield has asked me to marry him."

"When was this?"

"Oh, only today."

"And you're going to?"

"I think so. . . . Why do I say that? Of course I am."

"Quick work, Ann!"

"You mean I haven't known him long enough? Oh, but we're both quite sure."

"And you do know a good deal about him—through Colonel Grant. I'm very glad for you, my dear. You look very happy."

"I suppose it sounds very silly to you, Laura, but I do love him very much."

"Why should it sound silly? Yes, one can see that you love him."

"And he loves me."

"That also is apparent. Never have I seen a man look so exactly like a sheep!"

"Richard doesn't look like a sheep!"

"A man in love *always* looks like a sheep. It seems to be some law of nature."

"But you do like him, Laura?" Ann persisted.

This time Laura Whitstable did not answer so quickly. She said slowly:

"He's a very simple type of man, you know, Ann."

"Simple? Perhaps. But isn't that rather nice?"

"Well, it may have its difficulties. And he's sensitive, ultra-sensitive."

"It's clever of you to see that, Laura. Some people wouldn't."

"I'm not 'some people.' " She hesitated a moment and then said: "Have you told Sarah yet?"

"No, of course not. I told you. It only happened today."

"What I really meant was have you mentioned him in your letters—paved the way, so to speak?"

"No—no, not really." She paused before adding: "I shall have to write and tell her."

"Yes."

Again Ann hesitated before saying: "I don't think Sarah will mind very much, do you?"

"Difficult to say."

"She's always so very sweet to me. Nobody knows how sweet Sarah can be—without, I mean, ever saying anything. Of course—I suppose—" Ann looked pleadingly at her friend. "She may think it *funny*."

"Quite likely. Do you mind?"

"Oh, *I* don't mind. But Richard will."

"Yes—yes. Well, Richard will have to lump it, won't he? But I should certainly let Sarah know about it all before she comes back. It will give her a little time to get used to the idea. When are you thinking of getting married, by the way?"

"Richard wants us to get married as soon as possible. And there really isn't anything to wait for, is there?"

"Nothing at all. The sooner you get married the better, I should say."

"It's really rather fortunate—Richard's just got a job—with Hellner Bros. He knew one of the junior partners in Burma during the war. It's lucky, isn't it?"

"My dear, everything seems to be turning out very well." She said again gently: "I'm very glad for you."

Getting up, Laura Whitstable went over to Ann and kissed her.

"Now then—why the puckered brow?"

"It's just Sarah—hoping she won't mind."

"My dear Ann, whose life are you living, yours or Sarah's?"

"Mine, of course, but—"

"If Sarah minds, she minds! She'll get over it. She loves you, Ann."

"Oh, I know."

"It's very inconvenient to be loved. Nearly everyone has found that out, sooner or later. The fewer people who love you the less you will have to suffer. How fortunate it is for me that most people dislike me heartily, and the rest only feel a cheerful indifference."

"Laura, that's not true. I—"

"Good-bye, Ann. And don't force your Richard to say that he likes me. Actually he took a violent dislike to me. It's not of the least consequence."

That night, at a public dinner, the learned man sitting next to Dame Laura was chagrined at the end of his exposition of a revolutionary innovation in shock therapy to find her fixing him with a blank stare.

"You've not been listening," he exclaimed reproachfully.

"Sorry, David. I was thinking of a mother and daughter."

"Ah, a Case." He looked expectant.

"No, not a case. Friends."

"One of these possessive mothers, I suppose?"

"No," said Dame Laura. "In this case it's a possessive daughter."

Chapter five

1

"Well, Ann, my dear," said Geoffrey Fane. "I'm sure I congratulate you—or whatever one says on these occasions. Er —h'm. He's, if I may say so, a very lucky fellow—yes, a very lucky fellow. I've never met him, have I? I don't seem to recall the name."

"No, I only met him a few weeks ago."

Professor Fane peered at her mildly over the top of his glasses as was his habit.

"Dear me," he said disapprovingly. "Isn't this all rather sudden? Rather impetuous?"

"No, I don't think so."

"Among the Matawayala, there is a courtship period of a year and a half at least—"

"They must be a very cautious people. I thought savages obeyed primitive impulses."

"The Matawayala are very far from being savages," said Geoffrey Fane in a shocked voice. "Theirs is a very distinctive culture. Their marriage rites are curiously complicated. On the eve of the ceremony the bride's friends—er hum— well, perhaps better not to go into that. But it's really very interesting and seems to suggest that at one time the sacred ritual marriage of the Chief Priestess—no, I really must not run on. A wedding present now. What would you like as a wedding present, Ann?"

"You really don't need to give me a wedding present, Geoffrey."

"A piece of silver, usually, is it not? I seem to remember purchasing a silver mug—no, no, that was for a christening—spoons, perhaps? Or a toast-rack? Ah, I have it, a rose-bowl. But, Ann, my dear, you do know something *about* the fellow? I mean, he's vouched for—mutual friends, all that? Because one does read of such extraordinary things."

"He didn't pick me up on the pier, and I haven't insured my life in his favour."

Geoffrey Fane peered at her again anxiously and was relieved to find that she was laughing.

"That's all right, that's all right. Afraid you were annoyed with me. But one has to be careful. And how does the little girl take it?"

Ann's face clouded over for a moment.

"I wrote to Sarah—she's in Switzerland, you know—but I haven't had any answer. Of course, there's really been only just time for her to write, but I rather expected—" she broke off.

"Difficult to remember to answer letters. I find it increasingly so. Was asked to give a series of lectures in Oslo in March. Meant to answer it. Forgot all about it. Only found the letter yesterday—pocket of an old coat."

"Well, there's plenty of time still," said Ann consolingly.

Geoffrey Fane turned his mild blue eyes on her sadly.

"But the invitation was for last March, my dear Ann."

"Oh dear—but, Geoffrey, how could a letter stay all that time in a coat pocket?"

"It was my very old coat. One sleeve had become almost detached. That made it uncomfortable to wear. I—er—h'm—laid it aside."

"Somebody really ought to look after you, Geoffrey."

"I much prefer *not* to be looked after. I once had a very officious housekeeper, an excellent cook, but one of those inveterate tidiers-up. She actually threw away my notes on the Bulyano rain makers. An irreparable loss. Her excuse was that they were in the coal scuttle—but as I said to her: 'a coal scuttle is not a waste-paper basket, Mrs.—Mrs.—' whatever her name was. Women, I fear, have no sense of proportion. They attach an absurd importance to cleaning, which they perform as though it was a ritual act."

"Some people say it is, don't they? Laura Whitstable—you know her, of course—she quite horrified me by the sinister meaning she seemed to impute to people who wash their necks twice a day. Apparently the dirtier you are, the purer your heart!"

"In—deed? Well, I must be going." He sighed. "I shall miss you, Ann, I shall miss you more than I can say."

"But you're not losing me, Geoffrey. I'm not going away. Richard has a job in London. I'm sure you'll like him."

Geoffrey Fane sighed again.

"It will not be the same. No, no, when a pretty woman marries another man—" he squeezed her hand. "You have meant a great deal to me, Ann. I almost ventured to hope—but no, no, that could not have been. An old fogy such as I am. No, you would have been bored. But I am very devoted to you, Ann, and I wish you happiness with all my heart. Do you know what you have always reminded me of? Those lines in Homer."

He quoted with relish and at some length in Greek.

"There," he said, beaming.

"Thank you, Geoffrey," said Ann. "I don't know what it means—"

"It means that—"

"No, don't tell me. It couldn't possibly be as nice as it sounds. What a lovely language Greek is. Good-bye, dear Geoffrey, and thank you. . . . Don't forget your hat—that's not your umbrella, it's Sarah's sunshade—and—wait a minute—here's your brief-case."

She closed the front door after him.

Edith put her head out of the kitchen door.

"Helpless as a baby, isn't he?" she said. "And yet it's not that he's gaga, either. Clever in his own line, so I should think. Though I'd say as those native tribes as he's so keen about have downright nasty minds. That wooden figure he

brought you along I put in the back of the linen cupboard.
Needs a brasyair as well as a fig leaf. And yet the old professor himself hasn't got a nasty thought in his head. Not so
old either."

"He's forty-five."

"There you are. It's all this learning as has made him lose
his hair the way he has. My nephew's hair all came off in a
fever. Bald as an egg he was. Still, it grew again after a bit.
There's two letters there."

Ann picked them up.

"Returned postal packet?" Her face changed. "Oh, Edith,
it's my letter to Sarah. What a fool I am. I addressed it to
the hotel and no place name. I don't know what's the matter
with me just lately."

"I do," said Edith significantly.

"I do the stupidest things. . . . This other one is from
Dame Laura . . . oh, how sweet of her . . . I must ring
her up."

She went into the sitting-room and dialled.

"Laura? I just got your letter. It's really too kind of you.
There's nothing I'd like better than a Picasso. I've always
wanted to have a Picasso of my own. I shall put it over the
desk. You are kind to me. Oh, Laura, I've been such an idiot!
I wrote to Sarah telling her about everything—and now my
letter has come back. I just put Hotel des Alpes, Switzerland.
Can you *conceive* of my being so foolish?"

Dame Laura's deep voice said:

"H'm, interesting."

"What do you mean by interesting?"

"Just what I said."

"I know that tone of voice. You're getting at something.
You're hinting that I didn't really want Sarah to get my letter or something. It's that irritating theory of yours that all
mistakes are really deliberate."

"It isn't my theory specially."

"Well, anyway, it isn't true! Here I am with Sarah coming
home the day after tomorrow, and she won't know anything
at all and I shall have to tell her in so many words, which

really will be far more embarrassing. I simply shan't know how to begin."

"Yes, that's what you have let yourself in for by not wanting Sarah to get that letter."

"But I did want her to get it. Don't be so annoying."

There was a chuckle at the other end of the wire.

Ann said crossly:

"Anyway, it's a ridiculous theory! Why, Geoffrey Fane has just been here. He's just found an invitation to lecture in Oslo last March which he mislaid a year ago. I suppose you'd say he mislaid that on purpose?"

"Did he want to lecture in Oslo?" inquired Dame Laura.

"I suppose—well, I don't know."

Dame Laura said "Interesting," in a malicious voice and rang off.

2

Richard Cauldfield bought a bunch of daffodils at the florist's on the corner.

He was in a happy frame of mind. After his first doubts he was settling into the routine of his new job. Merrick Hellner, his boss, he found sympathetic—and their friendship, begun in Burma, proved itself a stable thing in England. The work was not technical. It was a routine administrative job in which a knowledge of Burma and the East came in handy. Richard was not a brilliant man, but he was conscientious, hard-working, and had plenty of common sense.

The first discouragements of his return to England were forgotten. It was like beginning a new life with everything in his favour. Congenial work, a friendly and sympathetic employer and the near prospect of marrying the woman he loved.

Every day he marvelled afresh that Ann should care for him. How sweet she was, so gentle and so appealing! And yet, sometimes, when he had been led to lay down the law somewhat dogmatically, he would look up to see her regarding him with a mischievous smile. He had not often been laughed at, and at first he was not sure that he liked it — but he had to admit in the end that from Ann he could take it and rather enjoy it.

When Ann said: "Aren't we pompous, darling?" he would first frown and then join in the laugh and say: "Suppose I was laying down the law a bit." And once he had said to her: "You're very good for me, Ann. You make me much more human."

She had said quickly: "We're both good for each other."

"There's not much I can do for you—except look after you and take care of you."

"Don't look after me too much. Don't encourage my weaknesses."

"Your weaknesses? You haven't any."

"Oh yes, I have, Richard. I like people to be pleased with me. I don't like rubbing people up the wrong way. I don't like rows—or fusses."

"Thank goodness for that! I'd hate to have a quarrelsome wife always scrapping. I've seen some, I can tell you! It's the thing I admire about you most, Ann, your being always gentle and sweet tempered. Dearest, how happy we are going to be."

She said softly:

"Yes, I think we are."

Richard, she thought, had changed a good deal since the night she had first met him. He had no longer that rather aggressive manner of a man who is on the defensive. He was, as he had said himself, much more human. More sure of himself, and therefore more tolerant and friendly.

Richard took his daffodils and went up to the block of flats. Ann's flat was on the third floor. He went up in the lift after having been greeted affably by the porter who now knew him well by sight.

Edith opened the door to him and from the end of the passage he heard Ann's voice calling rather breathlessly:

"Edith—Edith, have you seen my bag? I've put it down somewhere."

"Good-afternoon, Edith," said Cauldfield as he stepped inside.

He was never quite at his ease with Edith and tried to mask the fact by an additional bonhomie that did not sound quite natural.

"Good-afternoon, sir," said Edith respectfully.

"Edith—" Ann's voice sounded urgently from the bedroom. "Didn't you hear me? Do *come!*"

She came out into the passage just as Edith said:

"It's Mr. Cauldfield, ma'am."

"Richard?" Ann came down the passage towards him looking surprised. She drew him into the sitting-room, saying over her shoulder to Edith: "You *must* find that bag. See if I left it in Sarah's room?"

"Lose your head next, you will," said Edith as she went off.

Richard frowned. Edith's freedom of speech offended his sense of decorum. Servants had not spoken so fifteen years ago.

"Richard—I didn't expect you today. I thought you were coming to lunch tomorrow."

She sounded taken aback, slightly uneasy.

"Tomorrow seemed a long way off," he said, smiling. "I brought you these."

As he handed her the daffodils and she exclaimed with pleasure he suddenly noticed that there was already a profusion of flowers in the room. A pot of hyacinths was on the low table by the fire and there were bowls of early tulips and of narcissus.

"You look very festive," he said.

"Of course. Sarah's coming home today."

"Oh yes—yes, so she is. Do you know I'd forgotten."

"Oh, Richard."

Her tone was reproachful. It was true, he had forgotten. He had known perfectly the day of her arrival, but when he and Ann had been at a theatre together the night before neither of them had referred to the fact. Yet it had been discussed between them and agreed that on the evening Sarah returned, she should have Ann to herself and that he should come to lunch on the following day to meet his stepdaughter to be.

"I'm sorry, Ann. Really it had slipped my memory. You seem very excited," he added with a faint note of disapproval.

"Well, homecomings are always rather special, don't you think?"

"I suppose so."

"I'm just going off to the station to meet her." She glanced at her watch. "Oh, it's all right. Anyway, I expect the boat train will be late. It usually is."

Edith marched into the room, carrying Ann's bag.

"In the linen cupboard—that's where you left it."

"Of course—when I was looking for those pillow-cases. You've put Sarah's own green sheets on her bed? You haven't forgotten?"

"Now, do I ever forget?"

"And you remembered the cigarettes?"

"Yes."

"And Toby and Jumbo?"

"Yes, yes, yes."

Shaking her head indulgently, Edith went out of the room.

"Edith," Ann called her back and held out the daffodils. "Put these in a vase, will you?"

"I'll be hard put to it to find one! Never mind, I'll find something."

She took the flowers and went out.

Richard said: "You're as excited as a child, Ann."

"Well, it's so lovely to think of seeing Sarah again."

He said teasingly, yet with a slight stiffness:

"How long is it since you've seen her—a whole three weeks?"

"I daresay I'm ridiculous," Ann smiled at him disarmingly, "but I do love Sarah very much. You wouldn't want me not to, would you?"

"Of course I wouldn't. I'm looking forward to meeting her."

"She's so impulsive and affectionate. I'm sure you'll get on together."

"I'm sure we shall."

He added, still smiling: "She's your daughter—so she's sure to be a very sweet person."

"How nice of you to say that, Richard." Resting her hands on his shoulders, she lifted her face to his. "Dear Richard," she murmured as she kissed him. Then she added: "You—you will be patient, won't you darling? I mean—you see our going to be married may be rather a shock to her. If only I hadn't been stupid about that letter."

"Now don't get rattled, dearest. You can trust me, you know. Sarah may take it a bit hard at first, but we must get her to see that it's really quite a good idea. I assure you that I shan't be offended by anything she says."

"Oh, she won't *say* anything. Sarah has very good manners. But she does so hate change of any kind."

"Well, cheer up, darling. After all, she can't forbid the banns, can she?"

Ann did not respond to his joke. She was still looking worried.

"If only I'd written at once—

Richard said, laughing outright:

"You look exactly like a little girl who's been caught stealing the jam! It will be all right, sweetheart. Sarah and I will soon make friends."

Ann looked at him doubtfully. The cheerful assurance of his manner struck the wrong note. She would have preferred him to be slightly more nervous.

Richard went on:

"Darling, you really must *not* let things worry you so!"

"I don't usually," Ann said.

"But you do. Here you are, dithering—when the whole thing is perfectly simple and straightforward."

Ann said: "It's just that I'm—well, *shy*. I don't exactly know what to say, how to put it."

"Why not just say: 'Sarah, this is Richard Cauldfield. I'm getting married to him in three weeks' time.' "

"Quite baldly—like that?" Ann smiled in spite of herself. Richard smiled back.

"Isn't it really the best way?"

"Perhaps it is." She hesitated. "What you don't realise is that I shall feel so—so frightfully silly."

"Silly?" he took her up sharply.

"One does feel silly telling one's grown-up daughter that one's going to be married."

"I really can't see why."

"I suppose because young people unconsciously consider you as having done with all that sort of thing. You're *old* to them. They think love—falling in love, I mean—is a monopoly of youth. It's bound to strike them as ridiculous that middle-aged people should fall in love and marry."

"Nothing ridiculous about it," said Richard sharply.

"Not to *us*, because we *are* middle-aged."

Richard frowned. His voice, when he spoke, had a slight edge of asperity to it.

"Now look here, Ann, I know you and Sarah are very devoted to each other. I daresay the girl may feel rather sore and jealous about me. I understand that, it's natural, and I'm prepared to make allowances for it. I daresay she'll dislike me a good deal at first—but she'll come round all right. She must be made to realise that you've a right to live your own life and find your own happiness."

A slight flush rose in Ann's cheek.

"Sarah won't grudge me my 'happiness,' as you call it," she said. "There's nothing mean or petty about Sarah. She's the most generous creature in the world."

"The truth is that you're working yourself up about nothing, Ann. For all you know Sarah may be quite glad you are getting married. It will leave her freer to lead her own life."

"Lead her own life," Ann repeated the phrase with scorn. "Really, Richard, you talk like a Victorian novel."

"The truth of it is, you mothers never want the bird to leave the nest."

"You're quite wrong, Richard—absolutely wrong."

"I don't want to annoy you, darling, but sometimes even the most devoted mother's affection can be too much of a good thing. Why, I remember when I was a young man. I was very fond of my father and my mother, but living with them was often quite maddening. Always asking me how late I was going to be and where I was going. 'Don't forget your key.' 'Try and not make a noise when you come in.' 'You forgot to turn out the hall light last time.' 'What, going out *again* tonight? You don't seem to care at all about your home after all we've done for you.' " He paused. "I *did* care for my home—but oh God, how I wanted just to feel free."

"I understand all that, of course."

"So you mustn't feel injured if it turns out that Sarah hankers after her independence more than you think. There are so many careers open to girls nowadays, remember."

"Sarah's not a career type."

"That's what you say—but most girls do have a job, remember."

"That's very largely a question of economic necessity, isn't it?"

"What do you mean?"

Ann said impatiently:

"You're about fifteen years behind the times, Richard. Once it was all the fashion to 'lead your own life' and 'go out into the world.' Girls still do it, but there's no glamour about it. With taxation and death duties and all the rest of it, a girl is usually wise to train for something. Sarah has no special bent. She's well up in modern languages and she's been having a course of flower decoration. A friend of ours runs a floral decorating shop and she's arranged for Sarah to work there. I think she'll quite enjoy it—but it's just a job and that's all there is to it. It's no use talking so grandly about all this independence stuff. Sarah loves her home and she's perfectly happy here."

"I'm sorry if I've upset you, Ann, but—"

He broke off as Edith poked her head in. Her face had the smug expression of someone who has heard more of what is going on than she intends to admit.

"I don't want to interrupt you, ma'am, but you do know what time it is?"

Ann glanced down at her watch.

"There's still plenty of—why, it's exactly the same time as when I looked last." She held the watch to her ear. "Richard

—it's stopped. What is the time really, Edith?"

"Twenty past the hour."

"Good heavens—I shall miss her. But boat trains are always late, aren't they? Where's my bag? Oh here. Lots of taxis now, thank goodness. No, Richard, don't come with me. Look here, stay and have tea with us. Yes, do. I mean it. I think it would be best. Really I do. I *must* go."

She rushed out of the room. The front door banged. The swing of her fur had whisked two tulips out of the bowl. Edith stooped to pick them up and rearranged them carefully in the bowl, saying as she did so:

"Tulips is Miss Sarah's favourite flower—always was—especially mauve ones."

Richard said with some irritation:

"This whole place seems to revolve round Miss Sarah."

Edith stole a swift glance at him. Her face remained imperturbable—disapproving. She said in her flat unemotional voice:

"Ah, she's got a way with her, Miss Sarah has. That you can't deny. I've often noticed as how there's young ladies who leave their things about, expect everything mended for them, run you off your feet clearing up after them—and yet there's nothing you won't do for them! There's others as gives no trouble at all, everything neat, no extra work made —and yet there you are, you don't seem to fancy them in the same way. Say what you like it's an unjust world. Only a crazy politician would talk about fair shares for all. Some has the kicks and some has the ha'pence, and that's the way it is."

She moved round the room as she spoke, setting one or two objects straight and shaking up one of the cushions.

Richard lit a cigarette. He said pleasantly:

"You've been with Mrs. Prentice a long time, haven't you, Edith?"

"More than twenty years. Twenty-two, it is. Come to her mother before Miss Ann married Mr. Prentice. He was a nice gentleman, he was."

Richard looked at her sharply. His ultra-sensitive ego

led him to imagine that there had been a faint emphasis on
the "he."

He said:

"Mrs. Prentice has told you that we are going to be married shortly?"

Edith nodded.

"Not that I needed telling," she said.

Richard said rather self-consciously, speaking pompously
because he was shy: "I—I hope we shall be good friends,
Edith."

Edith said rather gloomily:

"I hope so, too, sir."

Richard said, still speaking stiffly:

"I'm afraid it may mean extra work for you, but we
must get outside help—"

"I'm not fond of these women that come in. When I'm
on my own I know where I am. Yes, it will mean changes
having a gentleman in the house. Meals is different to begin
with."

"I'm really not a large eater," Richard assured her.

"It's the *kind* of meals," said Edith. "Gentlemen don't
hold with trays."

"Women hold with them a good deal too much."

"That may be," Edith admitted. In a peculiarly lugubrious
voice she added: "I'm not denying that a gentleman about
the place cheers things up as it were."

Richard felt almost fulsomely grateful.

"That's very nice of you, Edith," he said warmly.

"Oh, you can rely on me, sir. I shan't go leaving Mrs.
Prentice. Wouldn't leave her for anything. And anyway it's
never been my way to quit if there's trouble in the offing."

"Trouble? What do you mean by trouble?"

"Squalls."

Again Richard repeated what she had said.

"Squalls?"

Edith faced him with an unflinching eye.

"Nobody asked my advice," she said. "And I'm not one to
give it unasked, but I'll say this. If Miss Sarah had come
back home to find you both married, and the whole thing

over and done with, well, it might have been better, if you take my meaning."

The front door-bell rang and almost immediately the button was pressed again and again.

"And I know who that is right enough," said Edith.

She went out into the hall. As she opened the door two voices were heard, one male, one female. There was laughter and exclamations.

"Edith, you old pet." It was a girl's voice, a warm contralto. "Where's mother? Come on, Gerry. Shove those skis in the kitchen."

"Not in my kitchen, you don't."

"Where's mother?" repeated Sarah Prentice, coming into the sitting-room and talking over her shoulder.

She was a tall dark girl, and her vigour and exuberant vitality took Richard Cauldfield by surprise. He had seen photographs of Sarah about the flat, but a photograph can never represent life. He had expected a younger edition of Ann—a harder, more modern edition—but the same type. But Sarah Prentice resembled her gay and charming father. She was exotic and eager and her mere presence seemed to change the whole atmosphere of the flat.

"Oo, lovely tulips," she exclaimed, bending over the bowl. "They've got that faint lemony smell that is absolutely spring. I—"

Her eyes widened as she straightened up and saw Cauldfield.

He came forward, saying:

"My name's Richard Cauldfield."

Sarah shook hands with him prettily, inquiring politely:

"Are you waiting for mother?"

"I'm afraid she's only just gone to the station to meet you —let me see, five minutes ago."

"How idiotic of the pet! Why didn't Edith get her off in time? Edith!"

"Her watch had stopped."

"Mother's watches—Gerry— Where are you, Gerry?"

A young man with a rather good-looking discontented face looked in for a moment with a suitcase in each hand.

"Gerry, the human robot," he remarked. "Where do you want all these, Sarah? Why don't you have porters in these flats?"

"We do. But they're never about if you arrive with luggage. Take them all along to my room, Gerry. Oh, this is Mr. Lloyd. Mr.—er—"

"Cauldfield," said Richard.

Edith came in. Sarah caught hold of her and gave her a resounding kiss.

"Edith, it's lovely to see your dear old sourpuss face."

"Sourpuss face indeed," said Edith indignantly. "And don't go kissing me, Miss Sarah. You ought to know your place better than that."

"Don't be so cross, Edith. You know you're delighted to see me. How clean everything looks! It's all just the same. The chintzes and mother's shell box—oh, you've changed the sofa round. And the desk. It was over there."

"Your ma says it gives more space this way."

"No, I want it as it was. Gerry—Gerry, where are you?"

Gerry Lloyd entered saying: "What's the matter now?" Sarah was already tugging at the desk. Richard moved to help her, but Gerry said cheerfully: "Don't bother, sir, I'll do it. Where do you want it, Sarah?"

"Where it used to be. Over there."

When they had moved the desk and pushed the sofa back into its old position, Sarah gave a sigh and said:

"That's better."

"I'm not so sure about that," said Gerry, standing back critically.

"Well, I am," said Sarah. "I like everything to be just the same. Otherwise home isn't home. Where's the cushion with the birds on it, Edith?"

"Gone to be cleaned."

"Oh well, that's all right. I must go and see my room." She paused in the doorway to say: "Mix some drinks, Gerry. Give Mr. Coalfield one. You know where everything is."

"Sure thing." Gerry looked at Richard. "What will you have, sir? Martini, gin and orange? Pink gin?"

Richard moved with sudden decision.

"No, thanks very much. Nothing for me. I've got to be off."

"Won't you wait until Mrs. Prentice comes in?" Gerry had a likeable and charming manner. "I don't suppose she'll be long. As soon as she finds the train came in before she got there she'll come straight back."

"No, I must go. Tell Mrs. Prentice the—er—original appointment stands—for tomorrow."

He nodded to Gerry and went out into the hall. From Sarah's bedroom along the passage he could hear her voice talking in a rush of words to Edith.

Better, he thought, not to stay now. His and Ann's original plan had been the right one. She would tell Sarah tonight and tomorrow he would come to lunch and start to make friends with his future step-daughter.

He was disturbed because Sarah was not as he had pictured her. He had thought of her as over-mothered by Ann, as dependent on Ann. Her beauty and her vitality and her self-possession had startled him.

Up to now she had been a mere abstraction. Now she was reality.

Chapter six

Sarah came back into the drawing-room fastening up a brocaded house-gown.

"I had to get out of that ski-ing suit. I really want a bath. How dirty trains are! Have you got a drink for me, Gerry?"

"Here you are."

Sarah accepted the glass.

"Thanks. Has that man gone? That's a good job."

"Who was he?"

"Never saw him in my life," said Sarah. She laughed. "He must be one of Mother's pick-ups."

Edith came into the room to pull the curtains and Sarah said:

"Who was he, Edith?"

"A friend of your mother's, Miss Sarah," said Edith.

She gave the curtains a sharp pull and then went to the second window.

Sarah said cheerfully: "Time I came home to choose her friends for her."

Edith said: "Ah," and pulled the second curtain. Then she said, looking hard at Sarah: "You didn't take to him?"

"No, I didn't."

Edith muttered something and went out of the room.

"What did she say, Gerry?"

"I think she said it was a pity."

"How funny."

"Sounded cryptic."

"Oh, you know what Edith's like. Why doesn't Mother come? Why does she have to be so vague?"

"She's not usually very vague. At least, I shouldn't have said so."

"It was nice of you to come and meet me, Gerry. Sorry I never wrote, but you know what life is. How did you manage to get off from the office early enough to get to Victoria?"

There was a slight pause before Gerry said:

"Oh, it wasn't particularly difficult under the circumstances."

Sarah sat up in a very alert way and looked at him.

"Now then, Gerry, out with it. What's wrong?"

"Nothing. At least, things haven't worked out very well."

Sarah said accusingly: "You said you were going to be patient and keep your temper."

Gerry frowned.

"I know all that, darling, but you've no idea what it's been like. Good God, to come home from somewhere like Korea where it's pretty fair hell, but at least most of the fellows are decent chaps, and then to get caught up in a money-grubbing City office. You've no idea what Uncle Luke is like. Fat and pursy with little darting eyes like a pig's. 'Very glad to have you home, me boy.' " Gerry was a good mimic. He wheezed out the words in an unctuous asthmatic way. " 'Er—ah—I hope now all this excitement's over, you'll come into the office and er—ah—really put your back into things. We're—er—short-handed—I think I can say there are—er excellent prospects if you're really serious over the job. Of course you'll start at the bottom. No—er, favours— that's my motto. You've had a long spell of playing around —now we'll see if you can get down to it in earnest.' "

He got up and strolled about.

"Playing about—that's what the fat so-and-so calls active service in the Army. My word, I'd like to see him sniped at by a yellow Chinese Red soldier. These rich bleeders sitting on their arses in their offices, never thinking of anything but money—going on—"

"Oh, dry up, Gerry," said Sarah impatiently. "Your uncle just hasn't got any imagination. Anyway, you said yourself you've got to have a job and make some money. I daresay it's all very unpleasant, but what's the alternative? You're lucky, really, to have a rich uncle in the City. Most people would give their eyes to have one!"

"And why is he rich?" demanded Gerry. "Because he's rolling in the money that ought to have come to *me*. Why Great-uncle Harry left it to him instead of to my father who was the elder brother—"

"Never mind all that," said Sarah. "Anyway, by the time the money had come to you, there probably wouldn't have been any. It would all have gone in death duties."

"But it was unfair. You'll admit that?"

"Everything's always unfair," said Sarah. "But it's no good going on grousing about it. For one thing it makes you such a bore. One gets so tired of hearing nothing but people's hard-luck stories."

"I must say you're not awfully sympathetic, Sarah."

"No. You see what I believe in is absolute frankness. I think you ought either to make a gesture and get out of this job, or else stop grousing about it and just thank your stars you've got a rich uncle in the City with pig's eyes and asthma. Hullo, I do believe I hear mother at last."

Ann had just opened the door with her latch-key. She came running into the sitting-room.

"Sarah darling."

"Mother—at last." Sarah enveloped her mother in a big hug. "What have you been doing with yourself?"

"It's my watch. It had stopped."

"Well, Gerry met me, so that was something."

"Oh hullo, Gerry, I didn't see you."

Ann greeted him cheerfully, though inwardly she felt annoyed. She had so hoped that this Gerry business would peter out.

"Let's have a look at you, darling," said Sarah. "You're looking quite smart. That's a new hat, isn't it? You look very well, Mother."

"So do you. And so sunburnt."

"Sun on the snow. Edith's awfully disappointed I didn't come home all swathed in bandages. You'd have liked me to have broken a few bones, wouldn't you, Edith?"

Edith, who was bringing in the tea-tray, made no direct reply.

"I've brought in three cups," she said, "though I suppose Miss Sarah and Mr. Lloyd won't want any, seeing as they've been drinking gin."

"How dissipated you make it sound, Edith," said Sarah. "Anyway, we offered what's-his-name some. Who is he, Mother? A name like Cauliflower."

Edith said to Ann: "Mr. Cauldfield said as he couldn't wait, ma'am. He'll be along tomorrow as previously arranged."

"Who is Cauldfield, Mother, and why does he have to come tomorrow? I'm sure we don't want him."

Ann said quickly: "Have another drink, won't you Gerry?"

"No, thank you, Mrs. Prentice. I really must be getting along now. Good-bye, Sarah."

Sarah went out with him into the hall. He said:

"What about a film this evening. There's a good continental one at the Academy."

"Oh, what fun. No—perhaps I'd better not. After all, it's my first evening home. I think I ought to spend it with mother. The poor pet might be disappointed if I rushed out at once."

"I do think, Sarah, that you're a frightfully good daughter."

"Well, mother's really very sweet."

"Oh, I know she is."

"She asks a terrible lot of questions, of course. You know, who one's met and what one's done. But on the whole, for a mother, she's really quite sensible. I tell you what, Gerry, if I find it's all right, I'll give you a ring later."

Sarah went back into the sitting-room and started to nibble cakes.

"These are Edith's specials," she remarked. "Madly rich. I don't know how she gets hold of the stuff to make them with. Now, Mother, tell me all you've been doing. Have you been out with Colonel Grant and the rest of the boy friends, and been having a good time?"

"No—at least yes, in a way . . ."

Ann stopped. Sarah stared at her.

"Is anything the matter, Mother?"

"The matter? No. Why?"

"You look all queer."

"Do I?"

"Mother, there *is* something. You really do look awfully peculiar. Come on, tell me. I've never seen such a guilty expression. Come on, Mother, what have you been up to?"

"Nothing really—at least. Oh, Sarah, darling—you must believe that it won't make any difference. Everything will be just the same, only—"

Ann's voice faltered and died. "What a coward I am," she thought to herself. "Why does a daughter make you feel so shy about things?"

Meanwhile Sarah was staring at her. Suddenly she began to grin the friendliest fashion.

"I do believe . . . Come on, Mother, own up. Are you trying to break it to me gently that I'm going to have a steppapa?"

"Oh, Sarah." Ann gave a gasp of relief. "*How* did you guess?"

"It wasn't so difficult as all that. I never saw anyone in such a frightful dither. Did you think I'd mind?"

"I suppose I did. And you don't? Really?"

"No," said Sarah seriously. "Actually I think you're quite right. After all, father died sixteen years ago. You ought to have some kind of sex life before it's too late. You're just at what they call the dangerous age. And you're much too old-fashioned to have just an affair."

Ann looked rather helplessly at her daughter. She was thinking how differently everything was going from the way she had thought it would go.

"Yes," said Sarah nodding her head. "With you it *has* to be marriage."

"The dear absurd baby," thought Ann, but was careful to say nothing of the kind.

"You're really quite good-looking still," went on Sarah with the devastating candour of youth. "That's because you've got a good skin. But you'd look heaps nicer if you'd have your eyebrows plucked."

"I like my eyebrows," said Ann obstinately.

"You're really awfully attractive, darling," said Sarah. "I'm really surprised you haven't got off before. Who is it, by the way? I'll have three guesses. One, Colonel Grant, two, Professor Fane, three that melancholy Pole with the unpronounceable name. But I'm pretty sure it's Colonel Grant. He's been hammering away at you for years."

Ann said rather breathlessly:

"It isn't James Grant. It's—it's Richard Cauldfield."

"Who's Richard Cauld—Mother, not that man who was here just now?"

Ann nodded.

"But you can't, Mother. He's all pompous and dreadful."

"He's not dreadful at all," said Ann sharply.

"Really, Mother, you could do a lot better than that."

"Sarah, you don't know what you're talking about. I—I care for him very much."

"You mean you're in love with him?" Sarah was frankly incredulous. "You mean you've actually got a *passion* for him."

Again Ann nodded.

"You know," said Sarah. "I really can't take all this in."

Ann straightened her shoulders.

"You only saw Richard for a moment or two," she said. "When you know him better, I'm sure you'll like him very much."

"He looks so aggressive."

"That was because he was shy."

"Well," said Sarah slowly, "it's your funeral, of course."

Mother and daughter sat silent for some moments. They were both embarrassed.

"You know, Mother," said Sarah, breaking the silence, "you really do need someone to look after you. Just because I go away for a few weeks, you go and do something silly."

"Sarah!" Anger flared up in Ann. "You're very unkind."

"Sorry, darling, but I do believe in absolute frankness."

"Well, I don't think I do."

"How long has this been going on?" demanded Sarah.

In spite of herself Ann laughed.

"Really, Sarah, you sound just like a heavy father in some Victorian drama. I met Richard three weeks ago."

"Where?"

"With James Grant. James has known him for years. He's just come back from Burma."

"Has he got any money?"

Ann was both irritated and touched. How ridiculous the child was—so earnest in her questions. Controlling her irritation she said in a dry ironical voice:

"He has an independent income and is fully able to support me. He has a job with Hellner Bros., a big firm in the City. Really, Sarah, anyone would think that *I* was *your* daughter, not the other way about."

Sarah said seriously: "Well, somebody has got to look after you, darling. You're quite unfit to look after yourself. I'm very fond of you, and I don't want you to go and do something foolish. Is he a bachelor or divorced or a widower?"

"He lost his wife many years ago. She died having her first baby and the baby died too."

Sarah sighed and shook her head.

"I see it all now. That's how he got at you. You always fall for sob stuff."

"Do stop being absurd, Sarah!"

"Has he got sisters and a mother—all that sort of thing?"

"I don't think he's got any near relations."

"That's a blessing anyway. Has he got a house? Where are you going to live?"

"Here, I think. There's heaps of room and his work is in London. You won't really mind, will you, Sarah?"

"Oh, *I* shan't mind. I'm thinking entirely of you."

"Darling, it's very sweet of you. But I really do know my own business best. I'm quite sure that Richard and I are going to be very happy together."

"When are you thinking of actually getting married?"

"In three weeks' time."

"In three weeks? Oh, you can't marry him as soon as that."

"There doesn't seem any point in waiting."

"Oh please, darling. Do put it off a little. Give me a little time to—to get used to the idea. Please, Mother."

"I don't know . . . we'll have to see . . ."

"Six weeks. Make it six weeks."

"Nothing's really decided yet. Richard's coming to lunch tomorrow. You—Sarah—you will be nice to him, won't you?"

"Of course I shall be nice to him. What do you think?"

"Thank you, darling."

"Cheer up, Mother, there's nothing to worry about."

"I'm sure you'll really both get very fond of each other," said Ann, rather weakly.

Sarah was silent.

Ann said, again with that gust of sudden anger:

"You might at least try—"

"I've told you you needn't worry." Sarah added after a moment or two: "I suppose you'd rather I stopped in tonight?"

"Why? Do you want to go out?"

"I thought I might—but I don't want to leave you alone, Mother."

Ann smiled at her daughter, the old relationship reasserting its sway.

"Oh, I shan't be lonely. As a matter of fact, Laura asked me to go to a lecture—"

"How is the old battle-axe? As indefatigable as ever?"

"Oh yes, just the same. I said no to the lecture, but I can easily ring her up."

She could, just as easily, ring Richard up. . . . But her mind shied away from the prospect. Better keep away from Richard until after he and Sarah had met on the morrow.

"That's all right, then," said Sarah. "I'll ring up Gerry."

"Oh, is it Gerry you're going out with?"

Sarah said, rather defiantly:

"Yes. Why not?"

But Ann did not take up the challenge. She said mildly: "I just wondered. . . ."

Chapter seven

1

"Gerry?"

"Yes, Sarah?"

"I don't really want to see this film. Can we go somewhere and talk?"

"Of course. Shall we go and have something to eat?"

"Oh, I couldn't. Edith has absolutely stuffed me."

"We'll go and get a drink somewhere then."

He cast a swift glance at her, wondering what had upset her. It was not until they were settled with drinks in front of them that Sarah spoke. Then she plunged abruptly:

"Gerry, mother's getting married again."

"Whew!" He was genuinely surprised.

"Hadn't you any idea of it?" he asked.

"How could I? She only met him since I've been away."

"Quick work."

"Much too quick. In some ways mother has really no sense at all!"

"Who is it?"

"That man who was there this afternoon. His name's Cauliflower or something like that."

"Oh, *that* man."

"Yes. Don't you agree that he's really quite impossible?"

"Well, I didn't really notice him much," said Gerry considering. "He seemed quite an ordinary sort of chap."

"He's absolutely the wrong person for mother."

"I suppose she's the best judge of that," said Gerry mildly.

"No, she isn't. The trouble about mother is that she's *weak*. She gets sorry for people. Mother needs somebody to look after her."

"Apparently she thinks so too," said Gerry with a grin.

"Don't laugh, Gerry, this is serious. Cauliflower is the wrong type for mother."

"Well, that's her business."

"I've got to look after her. I've always felt that. I know much more about life than she does, and I'm twice as tough."

Gerry did not dispute the statement. On the whole he agreed with it. Nevertheless he was troubled.

He said slowly: "All the same, Sarah, if she wants to get married again—"

Sarah broke in quickly:

"Oh, I quite agree to *that*. Mother *ought* to marry again. I told her so. She's been starved, you know, of a proper sex life. But definitely not Cauliflower."

"You don't think—" Gerry stopped uncertainly.

"Don't think what?"

"That you might—well, feel the same about anyone?" He was slightly nervous—but he got the words out. "After all, you can't really know that Cauliflower is the wrong sort for her. You've not spoken two words to him. Don't you think that perhaps it's really that you are—" it took courage to get the last word out, but he achieved it—"er—jealous?"

Sarah was up in arms at once.

"Jealous? *Me?* You mean step-father stuff? My dear Gerry! Didn't I say to you long ago—before I went to

Switzerland—that mother ought to marry again?"

"Yes. But it's different," said Gerry with a flash of perception, "just saying things from when they really happen."

"I've not got a jealous nature," said Sarah. "It's only mother's happiness I'm thinking about," she added virtuously.

"If I was you I wouldn't go monkeying about with other people's lives," said Gerry decidedly.

"But it's my own *mother*."

"Well, she probably knows her own business best."

"I tell you, mother's *weak*."

"Anyway," said Gerry, "there isn't anything you can do about it."

He thought Sarah was making a lot of fuss about nothing. He was tired of Ann and her affairs and wanted to talk about himself.

He said abruptly:

"I'm thinking about clearing out."

"Clearing out of your uncle's office? Oh, Gerry."

"I really can't stick it any longer. There's the hell of a fuss every time I turn up a quarter of an hour late."

"Well, you have to be punctual in offices, don't you?"

"Miserable lot of stick-in-the-muds! Fumbling away over ledgers, thinking of nothing but money, morning, noon and night."

"But Gerry, if you chuck it, what will you do?"

"Oh, I'll find something," said Gerry airily.

"You've tried a lot of things already," said Sarah doubtfully.

"Meaning I always get the sack? Well, I'm not waiting for the sack this time."

"But Gerry, really, do you think you're wise?" Sarah looked at him with a worried, almost maternal, solicitude. "I mean he's your uncle and about the only relation you have, and you did say he was rolling."

"And if I behave prettily he may leave me all his money? I suppose that's what you mean."

"Well, you grouse enough about your Great-uncle what's-his-name not leaving his money to your father."

"If he'd had any decent family feelings I wouldn't need to go truckling to these City magnates. I think this whole country is rotten to the core. I've a good mind to clear out of it altogether."

"Go abroad somewhere?"

"Yes. Go somewhere where one has *scope*."

They were both silent, envisaging a nebulous life that had scope.

Sarah, whose feet were always more firmly on the ground than Gerry's were, said acutely:

"Can you do anything much without capital? You haven't got any capital, have you?"

"You know I haven't. Oh, I imagine there are all sorts of things one can do."

"Well, what can you do—actually?"

"Must you be so damned depressing, Sarah?"

"Sorry. What I mean is you haven't any particular training of any kind."

"I'm good at handling men, and at leading an outdoor life. Not cooped up in an office."

"Oh, Gerry," said Sarah and sighed.

"What's the matter?"

"I don't know. Life does seem difficult. All these wars have unsettled things so."

They stared gloomily in front of them.

Presently Gerry said magnanimously that he'd give his uncle another chance. Sarah applauded this decision.

"I'd better go home now," she said. "Mother will be back from her lecture."

"What was the lecture about?"

"I don't know. 'Where are we going and Why?' That sort of thing."

She got up. "Thank you, Gerry," she said. "You've been very helpful."

"Try not to be prejudiced, Sarah. If your mother likes this fellow and is going to be happy with him, that's the main thing."

"If mother's going to be happy with him, then it's quite all right."

"After all, you'll be getting married yourself—I suppose—one of these days . . ."

He said it without looking at her. Sarah stared with absorption at her handbag.

"Someday, I suppose," she murmured. "I'm not particularly keen. . . ."

Embarrassment with a pleasurable tinge to it hovered in the air between them. . . .

2

Ann felt relieved in her mind during lunch on the following day. Sarah was behaving beautifully. She greeted Richard pleasantly and made conversation politely during the meal.

Ann felt proud of her young daughter with her vivid face, and her pretty manners. She might have known she could rely on Sarah—Sarah would never let her down.

What she did wish was that Richard could show to better advantage. He was nervous, she realised that. He was anxious to make a good impression, and as is so often the case, his very anxiety told against him. His manner was didactic, almost pompous. Being anxious to appear at ease, he gave the impression of dominating the party. The very deference that Sarah showed to him, heightened the impression he made. He was over-positive in his statements and seemed to indicate that no opinion was possible but his own. It vexed Ann who knew only too well the very real diffidence that there was in his nature.

But how could Sarah perceive it? She was seeing the worst side of Richard, and it was so important that she should see the best. It made Ann herself nervous and ill at ease and that, she soon saw, annoyed Richard.

After the meal was over and coffee had been brought, she left them on the excuse of having a telephone call to make. There was an extension in her bedroom. She hoped that, left together, Richard might feel more at ease and show more of his true self. It was she who was really the irritant. Once she had removed herself, things might settle down.

After Sarah had given Richard his coffee, she offered a

few polite commonplaces and the conversation then petered out.

Richard braced himself. Frankness, he judged, was his best suit. He was favourably impressed on the whole with Sarah. She had shown no hostility. The great thing was to show her how well he understood the position. Before coming he had rehearsed what he meant to say. Like most things that have been rehearsed beforehand, they came out flatly and in an artificial manner. To make himself feel at ease he adopted a confident bonhomie that was wildly removed from his actual painful shyness.

"Look here, young lady, there are just one or two things I'd like to say to you."

"Oh, yes?" Sarah turned an attractive but at the moment quite expressionless face towards him. She waited politely and Richard felt more nervous still.

"I just want to say that I quite understand your feelings. This must all have come as a bit of a shock to you. You and your mother have always been very close. It's perfectly natural that you should resent somebody else coming into her life. You're bound to feel a bit sore and jealous about it."

Sarah said quickly in pleasant formal tones:

"Not at all, I assure you."

Unwary, Richard took no notice of what was, in effect, a warning.

He blundered on:

"As I say, that's all quite normal. I shan't hurry you. Be as cool to me as you please. When you decide you're ready to be friends, I'll be ready to meet you halfway. What you've got to think of is your mother's happiness."

"I do think of that," said Sarah.

"Up to now, she's done everything for you. Now it's *her* turn to be considered. You want her to be happy, I'm sure. And you've got to remember this: you've got your own life to lead—it's all in front of you. You've got your own friends and your own hopes and ambitions. If you were to marry, or take up some job, your mother would be left all alone. That would mean great loneliness for her. This is the moment when you've got to put her first and yourself last."

He paused. He thought he had put that rather well.

Sarah's voice, polite but with an almost imperceptible undercurrent of impertinence, broke into his self-congratulations.

"Do you often make public speeches?" she inquired.

Startled, he said: "Why?"

"I should think you would be rather good at it," Sarah murmured.

She was leaning back now in her chair admiring her nails. The fact that they were carmine red, a fashion which he disliked intensely, added to Richard's irritation. He had recognised now that he was meeting hostility.

With an effort he kept his temper. As a result he spoke in an almost patronising tone.

"Perhaps I was lecturing you a bit, my child. But I wanted to draw your attention to a few things you mightn't have considered. And I can assure you of one thing; your mother's not going to care for you any less because she cares for me, you know."

"Really? How kind of you to tell me so."

There was no doubt of the hostility now.

If Richard had abandoned his defences, if he had said simply:

"I'm making an awful mess of this, Sarah. I'm shy and unhappy and it makes me say all the wrong things, but I'm terribly fond of Ann and I do want you to like me if you possibly can," it might perhaps have melted Sarah's defences, since she was at heart a generous creature.

But instead, his tone stiffened.

"Young people," he said, "are inclined to be selfish. They don't usually think of anybody but themselves. But you've got to think of your mother's happiness. She's a right to a life of her own, and a right to take happiness when she finds it. She needs someone to look after her and protect her."

Sarah raised her eyes and looked him full in the face. The look in her eyes puzzled him. It was hard and there was a kind of calculation about it.

"I couldn't agree with you more," she said unexpectedly.

Ann came back into the room rather nervously.

"Any coffee left?" she asked.

Sarah poured out a cup carefully. She rose to her feet and handed the cup to her mother.

"There you are, Mother," she said. "You came back at just the right minute. We've had our little talk."

She walked out of the room. Ann looked inquiringly at Richard. His face was rather red.

"Your daughter," he said, "has made up her mind not to like me."

"Be patient with her, Richard, please be patient."

"Don't worry, Ann, I'm perfectly prepared to be patient."

"You see, it has come to her as rather a shock."

"Quite."

"Sarah has really a very loving heart. She's such a dear child, really."

Richard did not reply. He considered Sarah an odious young woman, but he could not very well tell her mother so.

"It will all work out," he said reassuringly.

"I'm sure it will. It only needs *time*."

They were both unhappy and they did not know quite what to say next.

3

Sarah had gone to her bedroom. With unseeing eyes she took clothes out of the wardrobe and spread them out on the bed.

Edith came in. "What are you doing, Miss Sarah?"

"Oh, looking through my things. Perhaps they need cleaning. Or mending or something."

"I've seen to all that. You've no need to bother."

Sarah did not reply. Edith took a quick look at her. She saw the tears welling up in Sarah's eyes."

"There, there, now, don't take on so."

"He's odious, Edith, quite odious. How could mother? Oh, everything's ruined, spoilt—nothing will ever be the same again!"

"Now, now, Miss Sarah. It's no good working yourself up.

Least said, soonest mended. What can't be cured must be endured."

Sarah laughed wildly.

"A stitch in time saves nine! And rolling stones gather no moss! Go away, Edith. Do go away."

Edith shook her head sympathetically and went away, shutting the door.

Sarah cried passionately, like a child. She was torn with misery. Like a child she saw blackness everywhere with nothing to redeem the gloom.

Under her breath she sobbed: "Oh, Mother, Mother, *Mother.* . . ."

Chapter eight

1

"Oh, Laura, how pleased I am to see you."

Laura Whitstable sat down in an upright chair. She never lolled.

"Well, Ann, how's everything going?"

Ann sighed.

"Sarah's being rather difficult, I'm afraid."

"Well, that was to be expected, wasn't it?"

Laura Whitstable spoke with casual cheerfulness. But she looked at Ann with some concern.

"You're not looking very fit, my dear."

"I know. I don't sleep well and I get headaches."

"Don't take things too seriously."

"It's all very well to say that, Laura. You've no idea what it's like the whole time." Ann spoke fretfully. "The moment Sarah and Richard are left together for a moment, they quarrel."

"Sarah's jealous, of course."

"I'm afraid so."

"Well, as I said, that was to be expected. Sarah is still very much of a child. All children resent their mothers giving time and attention to somebody else. Surely you were prepared for that, Ann?"

"Yes, in a way. Although Sarah has always seemed so very detached and grown-up. Still, as you say, I was prepared for that. What I wasn't prepared for was Richard being jealous of Sarah."

"You expected Sarah to make a fool of herself, but thought that Richard might have a little more sense?"

"Yes."

"He's a man who's fundamentally unsure of himself. A more self-confident man would just laugh and tell Sarah to go to the devil."

Ann rubbed her forehead in an exasperated gesture.

"Really, Laura, you've no idea what it's like! They fall out about the silliest things and then they look at me to see which side I'm going to take."

"Very interesting."

"Very interesting to you—but it's not much fun for me."

"Which side *do* you take?"

"Neither if I can help it. But sometimes—"

"Yes, Ann?"

Ann was silent for a moment, then she said:

"You see, Laura, Sarah is cleverer than Richard about it all."

"In what way do you mean?"

"Well, Sarah's manner is always quite correct—outwardly. Polite, you know, and all that. But she knows how to get under Richard's skin. She—she torments him. And then he bursts out and becomes quite unreasonable. Oh, why can't they like each other?"

"Because there's a real natural antipathy between them, I should suppose. Do you agree with that? Or do you think it's only jealousy about you?"

"I'm afraid you may be right, Laura."

"What sort of things do they quarrel about?"

"The silliest things. For instance, you remember that I changed the furniture round, moved the desk and the sofa—and then Sarah moved it all back again, because she hates things changed . . . Well, Richard said suddenly one day:

'I thought you liked the desk over there, Ann.' I said I did think it gave more space. Then Sarah said, 'Well, I like it the way it always was.' And immediately Richard said in that domineering tone he sometimes puts on: 'It's not a question of what *you* like, Sarah, it's a question of what your mother likes. We'll arrange it the way she likes here and now.' And he moved the desk then and there and said to me: 'That's how you want it, isn't it?' So I more or less had to say 'Yes.' And he turned on Sarah and said: 'Any objections, young woman?' And Sarah looked at him and said quite quietly and politely: 'Oh, no. It's for mother to say. I don't count.' And you know, Laura, although I'd been backing up Richard, I really *felt* with Sarah. She loves her home and all the things in it—and Richard doesn't understand how she feels in the least. Oh dear, I don't know what to do."

"Yes, it's trying for you."

"I suppose it will wear off?"

Ann looked at her friend hopefully.

"I shouldn't count on that."

"I must say, you're not very comforting, Laura!"

"No good telling oneself fairy stories."

"It's really too unkind of them both. They ought to realise how unhappy they are making me. I really do feel *ill*."

"Self-pity won't help you, Ann. It never helps anybody."

"But I'm so unhappy."

"So are they, my dear. Give your pity to them. Sarah, poor child, is desperately miserable—and so, I imagine, is Richard."

"Oh dear, and we were so happy together until Sarah came home."

Dame Laura raised her eyebrows slightly. She was silent for a moment or two. Then she said: "You are getting married—when?"

"March 13th."

"Nearly two weeks still. You put it off—why?"

"Sarah begged me to. She said it would give her more time to get used to the idea. She went on and on at me until I gave way."

"Sarah . . . I see. And Richard was annoyed?"

"Of course he was annoyed. He was really very angry. He keeps saying that I've always spoilt Sarah. Laura, do you think that is true?"

"No, I don't. For all your love for Sarah you've never indulged her unduly. And up to now Sarah has always shown a reasonable consideration for you—as much, that is, as any egotistical young creature can."

"Laura, do you think I ought to—"

She stopped.

"Do I think you ought to do what?"

"Oh, nothing. But sometimes I feel I can't stand much more of this . . ."

She broke off as there was a sound of the front door of the flat opening. Sarah came into the room and looked pleased to see Laura Whitstable.

"Oh, Laura, I didn't know you were here."

"How's my godchild?"

Sarah came over and kissed her. Her cheek was fresh and cold from the outside air.

"I'm fine."

Murmuring something, Ann left the room. Sarah's eyes followed her. As they returned and met Dame Laura's, Sarah flushed guiltily.

Laura Whitstable nodded her head vigorously.

"Yes, your mother's been crying."

Sarah looked virtuous and indignant.

"Well, it's not *my* fault."

"Isn't it? You're fond of your mother, aren't you?"

"I adore mother. You know I do."

"Then why make her unhappy?"

"But I don't. I don't do *anything*."

"You quarrel with Richard, don't you?"

"Oh, *that!* Nobody could help it! He's impossible! If only mother could realise how impossible he is! I really think she will some day."

Laura Whitstable said:

"*Must* you try and arrange other people's lives for them, Sarah? In my young days it was parents who were accused of doing that to their children. Nowadays, it seems, it's the other way round."

Sarah sat down on the arm of Laura Whitstable's chair. Her manner was confiding.

"But I'm very worried," she said. "She's not going to be happy with him, you see."

"It's none of your business, Sarah."

"But I can't held *minding* about it. Because I don't want mother to be unhappy. And she will be. Mother's so—so helpless. She needs looking after."

Laura Whitstable imprisoned Sarah's two sunburnt hands in hers. She spoke with a forcefulness that startled Sarah into attention and something like alarm.

"Now listen, Sarah. Listen to me. *Be careful.* Be *very* careful."

"What do you mean?"

Again Laura spoke with emphasis.

"Be very careful you don't let your mother do something she'll regret all her life."

"That's just what I—"

Laura swept on.

"I'm warning you. No one else will." She gave a sudden prolonged sniff, drawing in air through her nose. "I smell something in the air, Sarah, and I'll tell you what it is. *It's the smell of a burnt offering*—and I don't like burnt offerings."

Before they could say any more Edith opened the door and announced:

"Mr. Lloyd."

Sarah jumped up.

"Hullo, Gerry." She turned to Laura Whitstable. "This is Gerry Lloyd. My godmother, Dame Laura Whitstable."

Gerry shook hands and said:

"I believe I heard you on the wireless last night."

"How gratifying."

"Giving the second talk in the series 'How to Be Alive Today.' I was much impressed."

"None of your impudence," said Dame Laura, looking at him with a sudden twinkle.

"No, but I was, really. You seemed to have all the answers."

"Ah," said Dame Laura. "It's always easier to tell someone how to make a cake than to do it yourself. It's also much more enjoyable. Bad for the character, though. I am well aware that I get more odious every day."

"Oh, you don't," said Sarah.

"Yes, I do, child. I've almost reached the point of giving people good advice—an unpardonable sin. I shall go and find your mother now, Sarah."

2

As soon as Laura Whitstable had left the room, Gerry said:

"I'm getting out of this country, Sarah."

Sarah stared at him, stricken.

"Oh, Gerry—when?"

"Practically at once. Next Thursday."

"Where?"

"South Africa."

"But that's a long way," cried Sarah.

"It is rather."

"You won't come back for years and years!"

"Probably not."

"What are you going to do there?"

"Grow oranges. I'm going in with a couple of other chaps. Ought to be quite fun."

"Oh, Gerry, *must* you go?"

"Well, I'm fed up with this country. It's too tame and too smug. It's got no use for me and I haven't got any use for it."

"What about your uncle?"

"Oh, we're no longer on speaking terms; Aunt Lena's been quite kind, though. Gave me a cheque and some patent stuff for snake bites."

He grinned.

"But do you *know* anything about growing oranges, Gerry?"

"Nothing whatever, but I imagine one soon picks it up."
Sarah sighed.

"I shall miss you. . . ."

"I don't suppose you will—not for long." Gerry spoke
rather gruffly, avoiding looking at her. "If one's away at the
other side of the world, people soon forget one."

"No, they don't. . . ."

He gave her a quick glance.

"Don't they?"

Sarah shook her head.

They looked away from each other, embarrassed.

"It's been fun—going about together," said Gerry.

"Yes . . ."

"People do quite well with oranges sometimes."

"I expect they do."

Gerry said, choosing his words carefully:

"I believe it's quite a cheery life—for a woman, I mean.
Good climate—and plenty of servants—all that."

"Yes."

"But I suppose you'll go marrying some fellow . . ."

"Oh, no." Sarah shook her head. "It's a great mistake to
marry too young. I don't mean to get married for ages."

"You think that—but some swine or other will make you
change your mind," said Gerry gloomily.

"I've got a very cold nature," said Sarah reassuringly.

They stood, awkwardly, not looking at each other. Then
Gerry, his face very pale, said in a choked voice:

"Darling Sarah—I'm crazy about you. You do know
that?"

"Are you?"

Slowly, as though unwillingly, they drew closer together.
Gerry's arms went round her. Timidly, wonderingly, they
kissed. . . .

Strange, Gerry thought, that he should be so clumsy. He
had been a gay young man and had had plenty of experience
with girls. But this wasn't "girls," this was his own darling
Sarah. . . .

"Gerry."

"Sarah . . ."

He kissed her again.

"You won't forget, darling Sarah, will you? All the amusing times we've had—and everything?"

"Of course I won't forget."

"You'll write to me?"

"I've got rather a thing about writing letters."

"But you'll write to me. Please, darling. I shall be so lonely. . . ."

Sarah pulled away from him and gave a shaky little laugh.

"You won't be lonely. There'll be lots of girls."

"If there are they'll be a lousy lot, I expect. But I rather imagine there will be nothing but oranges."

"You'd better send me a case from time to time."

"I will indeed. Oh, Sarah, I'd do anything for you."

"Well then, work hard. Make a success of your old orange farm."

"I will. I swear I will."

Sarah sighed.

"I wish you hadn't got to go just now," she said. "It's been such a comfort having you to talk things over with."

"How's Cauliflower? Do you like him any better?"

"No, I don't. We never stop having rows. But," her voice was triumphant, "I think I'm winning, Gerry!"

Gerry looked at her uncomfortably.

"You mean your mother—"

"I think she's beginning to see how impossible he is."

Sarah nodded her head in triumph.

Gerry looked more uncomfortable still.

"Sarah, I wish you wouldn't, somehow—"

"Not fight Cauliflower? I shall fight him tooth and nail! I won't give up. Mother's *got* to be saved."

"I wish you wouldn't interfere, Sarah. Your mother must know herself what she wants."

"I told you before, mother's weak. She gets sorry for people and her judgment goes. I'm saving her from making an unhappy marriage."

Gerry took his courage in both hands.

"Well, I still think you're just jealous."

Sarah cast him a furious look.

"All right! If that's what you think! You'd better go now."

"Now don't be mad with me. I daresay you know what you're doing."

"Of course I know," said Sarah.

3

Ann was in her bedroom sitting in front of the dressing-table when Laura Whitstable came in.

"Feeling better now, my dear?"

"Yes. It was really very stupid of me. I mustn't let these things get on my nerves."

"A young man has just arrived. Gerald Lloyd. Is that the one——"

"Yes. What did you think of him?"

"Sarah's in love with him, of course."

Ann looked troubled. "Oh dear, I do hope not."

"No good your hoping."

"It can't come to anything, you see."

"He's thoroughly unsatisfactory, is he?"

Ann sighed. "I'm afraid so. He never sticks to anything. He's attractive. One can't help liking him but——"

"No stability?"

"One just feels he will never make good *anywhere*. Sarah is always saying what hard luck he's had, but I don't think it's only that." She went on: "Sarah knows so many really nice men, too."

"And finds them dull, I suppose. Nice capable girls—and Sarah is really very capable—are always attracted to detrimentals. It seems a law of nature. I must confess that I found the young man attractive myself."

"Even you, Laura?"

"I have my womanly weaknesses, Ann. Good-night, my dear. Good luck to you."

4

Richard arrived at the flat just before eight. He was to dine there with Ann. Sarah was going out to a dinner and dance.

She was in the sitting-room when he arrived, painting her nails. There was a smell of pear-drops in the air. She looked up and said: "Hullo, Richard," and then resumed operations. Richard watched her with irritation. He was rather dismayed himself at the increasing dislike he felt for Sarah. He had meant so well, had seen himself as the kindly and friendly step-father, indulgent—almost fond. He had been prepared for suspicion at first, but had seen himself easily overcoming childish prejudices.

Instead it seemed to him that it was Sarah and not he who was in command of the situation. Her cool disdain and dislike pierced his sensitive skin and both wounded and humiliated him. Richard had never thought very much of himself, Sarah's treatment lowered his self-esteem still further. All his efforts, first to placate, then to dominate her, had been disastrous. He always seemed to say and do the wrong thing. Behind his dislike of Sarah there was growing, too, a rising irritation with Ann. Ann should support him. Ann should turn on Sarah and put her in her place, Ann should be on his side. Her efforts to play peacemaker, to steer a middle course, annoyed him. That sort of thing was no earthly use, and Ann ought to realise the fact!

Sarah stretched out a hand to dry, turning it this way and that.

Aware that it would have been better to say nothing, Richard could not stop himself remarking:

"Looks as though you'd dipped your fingers in blood. I can't think why you girls have to put that stuff on your nails."

"Can't you?"

Seeking for some safer topic, Richard went on:

"I met your friend young Lloyd this evening. He told me he was going out to South Africa."

"He's going on Thursday."

"He'll have to put his back into it if he wants to make a success out there. It's no place for a man who doesn't fancy working."

"I suppose you know all about South Africa?"

"All these places are much the same. They need men with guts."

"Gerry has plenty of guts," said Sarah, adding, "if you *must* use that expression."

"What's wrong with it?"

Sarah raised her head and gave him a cool stare.

"I just think it's rather disgusting—that's all," she said.

Richard's face went red.

"It's a pity your mother didn't bring you up to have better manners," he said.

"Was I rude?" Her eyes opened in an innocent stare. "I'm *so* sorry."

Her exaggerated apology did nothing to soothe him.

He asked abruptly:

"Where's your mother?"

"She's changing. She'll be here in a minute."

Sarah opened her bag and studied her face carefully. She began to touch it up, repainting her lips, applying eyebrow pencil. She had really made up her face some time ago. Her actions now were calculated to annoy Richard. She knew that he had a queer old-fashioned dislike of seeing a woman make up her face in public.

Trying to speak facetiously, Richard said:

"Come now, Sarah, don't overdo it."

She lowered the mirror she was holding and said:

"What do you mean?"

"I mean the paint and powder. Men don't really like such a lot of make-up, I can assure you. You simply make yourself look—"

"Like a tart, I suppose you mean?"

Richard said angrily:

"I didn't say so."

"But you meant it." Sarah dashed the make-up implements back in her bag. "Anyway, what the hell business is it of yours?"

"Look here, Sarah—"

"What I put on my face is my own business. It's no business of yours, you interfering Nosey Parker."

Sarah was trembling with rage, half crying.

Richard lost his temper thoroughly. He shouted at her:

"Of all the insufferable, bad-tempered little vixens. You're absolutely impossible!"

At that moment Ann came in. She stopped in the doorway and said wearily: "Oh dear, what's the matter *now?*"

Sarah rushed out past her. Ann looked at Richard.

"I was just telling her that she puts too much make-up on her face."

Ann gave a sharp exasperated sigh.

"Really, Richard, I do think you might have a little more sense. What earthly business is it of yours?"

Richard paced up and down angrily.

"Oh, very well. If you like your daughter going out looking like a tart."

"Sarah doesn't look like a tart," said Ann sharply. "What a horrid thing to say. All girls use make-up nowadays. You're so old-fashioned in your ideas, Richard."

"Old-fashioned! Out-of-date!—You don't think much of me, do you, Ann?"

"Oh, Richard, must we quarrel? Don't you realise that in saying what you did about Sarah, you're really criticising *me?*"

"I can't say I think you're a particularly judicious mother. Not if Sarah is a specimen of your bringing up."

"That's a cruel thing to say and it's not true. There's nothing wrong with Sarah."

Richard flung himself down on a sofa.

"God help a man who marries a woman with an only daughter," he said.

Ann's eyes filled with tears.

"You knew about Sarah when you asked me to marry you. I told you how much I loved her and all she meant to me."

"I didn't know you were absolutely besotted about her! It's Sarah, Sarah, Sarah with you from morning to night!"

"Oh dear," said Ann. She went over to him and sat down beside him. "Richard, do try to be reasonable. I did think Sarah might be jealous of you—but I didn't think you'd be jealous of Sarah."

"I'm not jealous of Sarah," said Richard sulkily.

"But darling, you are."

"You always put Sarah first."

"Oh dear." Ann lay back helplessly and shut her eyes. "I really don't know what to do."

"Where do I come in? Nowhere. I simply don't count with you. You put off our marriage—simply because Sarah asked you to—"

"I wanted to give her a little more time to get used to the idea."

"Is she any more used to it now? She spends her whole time doing every earthly thing she can to annoy me."

"I know she's been difficult—but really, Richard, I do think you exaggerate. Poor Sarah can hardly say a word without your flying into a rage."

"Poor Sarah. Poor Sarah. You see? That's what you feel!"

"After all, Richard, Sarah's very little more than a child. One makes allowances for her. But you're a man—an adult human being."

Richard said suddenly, disarmingly:

"It's because I love you so, Ann."

"Oh, my dear."

"We were so happy together—before Sarah came home."

"I know. . . ."

"And now—all the time I seem to be losing you."

"But you're not losing me, Richard."

"Ann, dearest—you do still love me."

Ann said with sudden passion:

"More than ever, Richard. More than ever."

5

Dinner was a successful meal. Edith had taken pains with it, and the flat, with Sarah's tempestuous influence removed, was once again the peaceful setting it had been before.

Richard and Ann talked together, laughed, reminded each other of past incidents, and to both of them it was a welcome halcyon calm.

It was after they had returned to the drawing-room and

had finished their coffee and Benedictine that Richard said:

"This has been a wonderful evening. So peaceful. Ann dearest, if it could always be like this."

"But it will be, Richard."

"You don't really mean that, Ann. You know, I've been thinking things over. Truth's an unpleasant thing, but it's got to be faced. Quite frankly, I'm afraid that Sarah and I are never going to hit it off. If the three of us try to live together, life's going to be impossible. In fact, there's only one thing to be done."

"What do you mean?"

"To put it bluntly, Sarah's got to get out of here."

"No, Richard. That's impossible."

"When girls aren't happy at home, they go and live on their own."

"Sarah's only nineteen, Richard."

"There are places where girls can live. Hostels. Or as a P.G. with a suitable family."

Ann shook her head decidedly.

"I don't think you realise what you are suggesting. You are suggesting that because I want to marry again, I turn out my young daughter—turn her out of her home."

"Girls like being independent and living on their own."

"Sarah doesn't. It's not a question of her wanting to go off on her own. This is her home, Richard. She's not even of age."

"Well, *I* think it's a good sound scheme. We can give her a good allowance to live on—I'll contribute. She needn't feel skimped. She'll be happy on *her* own, and we'll be happy on *our* own. I can't see anything wrong with the plan."

"You're assuming that Sarah *is* going to be happy on her own?"

"She'll enjoy it. I tell you girls like independence."

"You don't know anything about girls, Richard. All you're thinking of is what *you* want."

"I'm suggesting what I think is a perfectly reasonable solution."

Ann said slowly: "You said before dinner that I put Sarah

first. In a way, Richard, that's true. . . . It's not a question of which of you I love best. But when I consider you both—I know that it's Sarah whose interests have to come before yours. Because you see, Richard, Sarah is my responsibility. I've not done with that responsibility until Sarah is fully a woman—and she *isn't* fully a woman yet."

"Mothers never want their children to grow up."

"That's sometimes true, but I honestly don't think it's true of me and Sarah. I see, what you can't possibly see—that Sarah is still very young and defenceless."

Richard snorted.

"Defenceless!"

"Yes, that's just what I mean. She's unsure of herself, unsure of life. When she's ready to go out into the world, she'll *want* to go—and then I'll be only too ready to help her. But she's *not* ready."

Richard sighed. He said:

"I suppose one simply can't argue with mothers."

Ann said with unsuspected firmness:

"I'm not going to turn my daughter out of her home. To do that, when she didn't want to go, would be wicked."

"Well, if you feel so strongly about it."

"Oh, I do. But, Richard dear, if you will only have patience. Don't you see, it's not *you* who are the outsider, it's Sarah. And she feels it. But I know that, in time, she will learn to make friends with you. Because she really does love me, Richard. And, in the end, she won't want me to be unhappy."

Richard looked at her with a faintly quizzical smile.

"My sweet Ann, what an incurable wishful thinker you are."

She moved into the circle of his arm.

"Dear Richard—I love you. . . . Oh dear, I wish I hadn't got such a headache. . . ."

"I'll get you some aspirin. . . ."

It occurred to him that every conversation he had with Ann now ended in aspirin.

Chapter nine

1

For two days there was an unexpected welcome peace. It
encouraged Ann. Things after all were not so bad. In time,
as she had said, everything would settle down. Her appeal to
Richard had been successful. In a week's time they would be
married—and after that, it seemed to her, life would be more
normal. Sarah would surely cease to resent Richard so much,
and would find more interest in outside matters.

"I really feel much better today," she observed to Edith.

It occurred to her that a day passing without a headache
was now quite a phenomenon.

"Bit of a lull in the storm, as you might say," agreed Edith.
"Just like cat and dog, Miss Sarah and Mr. Cauldfield. Taken
what you might call a real natural dislike to each other."

"I think Sarah's getting over it a bit, though, don't you?"

"I shouldn't buoy yourself up with false hopes if I was you,
ma'am," said Edith gloomily.

"But it can't go on like that always?"

"I shouldn't bank on that."

Edith, thought Ann, was always gloomy! She enjoyed
predicting disasters.

"It *has* been better just lately," she insisted.

"Ah, because Mr. Cauldfield's been here mostly in the day-
time when Miss Sarah's at her flower business, and she's
had you to herself in the evenings. Besides, she's taken up
with that Mr. Gerry going off to foreign parts. But once
you're married, you'll have both of them here together. Tear
you to pieces between them, they will."

"Oh, Edith." Dismay seized Ann. A horrible simile.

And so exactly what she had been feeling.

She said desperately: "I can't bear it. I *hate* scenes and
rows and always have."

"That's right. Quiet and sheltered you've always lived,

and that's the way it suits you."

"But what can I do about it? What would *you* do, Edith?"

Edith said with relish:

"No use repining. Taught as a child I was. *'This life is but a vale of tears.'* "

"If that's all you can suggest to console me!"

"These things are sent to try us," said Edith sententiously. "Now if only you were one of those ladies who enjoy rows! There's many that do. My uncle's second wife, for instance. Nothing she enjoys more than going at it hammer and tongs. Wicked tongue she's got—but there, once it's over, she bears no malice and never thinks twice about it again. Cleared the air, so to speak. Irish blood, I put it down to. Her mother came from Limerick. No spite in them, but always spoiling for a fight. Miss Sarah's got a bit of that. Mr. Prentice was half Irish, I remember your telling me. Likes to blow off steam, Miss Sarah does, but a better-hearted young lady never lived. If you ask me it's a good thing Mr. Gerry's taking himself off across the sea. He'll never settle down and go steady. Miss Sarah can do better than him."

"I'm afraid she's rather fond of him, Edith."

"I shouldn't worry. *Absence makes the heart grow fonder,* they say, but my Aunt Jane used to add on to that, 'of somebody else.' *Out of sight out of mind* is the truer proverb. Now don't you worry about her or anyone else. Here's that book you got from the library that you wanted so much to read, and I'll bring you in a nice cup of coffee and a biscuit or two. You enjoy yourself while you can."

The slightly sinister suggestion of the last three words was ignored by Ann. She said: "You're a great comfort, Edith."

On Thursday Gerry Lloyd left and Sarah came home that evening to have a worse quarrel than ever with Richard.

Ann left them and sought refuge in her own room. She lay there in the dark, her hands over her eyes, the fingers pressing on her aching forehead. Tears rolled down her cheeks.

She said to herself again and again under her breath: "I can't bear it. . . . I can't bear it. . . ."

Presently she heard the end of a sentence by Richard,

almost shouted as he stormed out of the sitting-room:

"—and your mother can't always get out of it by running away with one of her eternal headaches."

Then came the slam of the front door.

Sarah's footsteps sounded in the passage, coming slowly and hesitantly to her own room. Ann called out:

"Sarah."

The door opened. Sarah's voice, slightly conscience-stricken, said:

"All in the dark?"

"My head aches. Turn on the little lamp over in the corner."

Sarah did so. She came slowly towards the bed, her eyes averted. There was something forlorn and childish about her that struck at Ann's heart, although only a few minutes before she had felt violently angry with her.

"Sarah," said Ann. "Must you?"

"Must I what?"

"Quarrel with Richard the whole time? Haven't you got any feeling for me at all? Don't you realise how unhappy you're making me? Don't you want me to be happy?"

"Of course I want you to be happy. That's just *it!*"

"I don't understand you. You make me perfectly miserable. Sometimes I feel I can't go on. . . . Everything's so different."

"Yes, it's all different. He's spoilt everything. He wants to get me out of here. You won't let him make you send me away, will you?"

Ann was angry.

"Of course not. Who suggested such a thing?"

"He did. Just now. But you won't, will you? It's all like a bad dream." Suddenly Sarah's tears began to flow. "It's all gone wrong. Everything. Ever since I came back from Switzerland. Gerry's gone away—I shall probably never see him again. And you've turned against me—"

"I haven't turned against you! Don't say such things."

"Oh, Mother—Mother."

The girl flung herself down on her knees by the bed and sobbed uncontrollably.

She repeated at intervals that one word "Mother...."

2

On Ann's breakfast tray the next morning was a note from Richard.

> Dear Ann. Things really can't go on like this. We shall have to work out some kind of plan. I believe you will find Sarah more amenable than you think. Yours ever, Richard.

Ann frowned. Was Richard wilfully deceiving himself? Or had Sarah's outburst last night been largely hysterical? The latter was possible. Sarah, Ann felt sure, was suffering all the misery of calf love, and her first good-bye to the loved one. After all, since she disliked Richard so much, it might be that she really would be happier away from home. . . .

On an impulse Ann reached for the telephone and dialled Laura Whitstable's number.

"Laura? It's Ann."

"Good-morning. This is a very early call."

"Oh, I'm at my wit's end. My head never stops aching and I feel quite ill. Things just can't go on like this. I wanted to ask your advice."

"I don't give advice. It's a most dangerous thing to do."

Ann paid no attention.

"Listen, Laura, do you think—possibly—it would be a good thing—if—if Sarah went to live by herself—I mean shared a flat with a friend—or something like that?"

There was a moment's pause and then Dame Laura asked: "Does she want to?"

"Well—no—not exactly. I mean, it was just an *idea*."

"Who suggested it? Richard?"

"Well—yes."

"Very sensible."

"You do think it's sensible?" Ann said eagerly.

"I mean that it was very sensible from Richard's point of view. Richard knows what he wants—and goes for it."

"But what do *you* think?"

"I told you, Ann, I don't give advice. What does Sarah say?"

Ann hesitated.

"I haven't really discussed it with her—yet."

"But you've probably got some idea."

Ann said rather reluctantly: "I don't think she'd want to for a moment."

"Ah!"

"But perhaps I ought, really, to insist?"

"Why? To cure your headaches?"

"No, no," cried Ann, horrified. "I mean, entirely for her own happiness."

"That sounds magnificent! I always distrust noble sentiments. Elaborate, won't you?"

"Well, I've wondered whether perhaps I'm a rather clinging kind of mother. Whether it mightn't really be for Sarah's good to get away from me? So that she can develop her own personality."

"Yes, yes, very modern."

"Really, you know, I think she might quite *take* to the idea. I didn't at first, but now—Oh, do say what you think!"

"My poor Ann."

"Why do you say 'My poor Ann'?"

"You asked me what I thought."

"You're not being very helpful, Laura."

"In the sense you mean, I don't want to be."

"You see, Richard is really getting very hard to manage. He wrote me a kind of ultimatum this morning. . . . Soon he'll be asking me to choose between him and Sarah."

"And which would you choose?"

"Oh, don't, Laura. I didn't really mean it had come to that."

"It may do."

"Oh, you're maddening, Laura. You don't even try and help."

Ann banged down the receiver angrily.

3

At six o'clock that evening Richard Cauldfield rang up.

Edith answered the telephone.

"Mrs. Prentice in?"

"No, sir. She's out on that committee she goes to—an Old Ladies' Home or some such. She won't be back much before seven."

"And Miss Sarah?"

"Just come in. Do you want to speak to her?"

"No, I'll come round."

Richard covered the distance between his service flat and Ann's block of flats with a firm even tread. He had passed a sleepless night and had finally come to a definite resolution. Though a man who took a little time to make up his mind, once he had made it up, he stuck to his decision obstinately.

Things could not go on as they were. First Sarah and then Ann would have to be made to see that. That girl was wearing her mother out with her tantrums and her obstinacy! His poor tender Ann. But his thoughts of her were not entirely loving. Almost unrecognised, he felt a certain resentment against her. She was continually evading the point by her feminine artifices—her headaches, her collapse whenever a battle raged. . . . Ann had got to face up to things!

These two women. . . . All this feminine nonsense had got to *stop!*

He rang the bell, was admitted by Edith and went into the sitting-room. Sarah, a glass in her hand, turned from the mantelpiece.

"Good-evening, Richard."

"Good-evening, Sarah."

Sarah said with an effort:

"I'm sorry, Richard, about last night. I'm afraid I was rather rude."

"That's all right." Richard waved a magnanimous hand. "We'll say no more about it."

"Will you have a drink?"

"No, thanks."

"I'm afraid mother won't be in for some time. She's gone to—"

He interrupted:

"That's all right. It's you I came to see."

"Me?"

Sarah's eyes darkened and narrowed. She came forward and sat down, watching him suspiciously.

"I want to talk things over with you. It seems to me perfectly clear that we can't go on as we are. All this sparring and bickering. It's not fair on your mother for one thing. You care for your mother, I'm sure."

"Naturally," said Sarah unemotionally.

"Then, between us, we've got to give her a break. In a week's time she and I are getting married. When we come back from our honeymoon, what sort of life do you think it is going to be, the three of us living here in this flat?"

"Pretty fair hell, I should think."

"You see? You recognise it yourself. Now I want to say right at the start that I don't put all the blame on you."

"That's very magnanimous of you, Richard," said Sarah.

Her tone was earnest and polite. He still did not know Sarah well enough to recognise a danger signal.

"It's unfortunate that we just don't get on. To be frank, you dislike me."

"If you must have it, yes, I do."

"That's all right. On my side, I'm not particularly fond of you."

"You hate me like poison," said Sarah.

"Oh, come now," said Richard, "I wouldn't put it as strongly as that."

"I would."

"Well, let's put it this way. We dislike each other. It doesn't matter much to me whether you like me or not. It's your mother I'm marrying, not you. I've tried to make friends with you but you won't have it. . . . So we've got to find a solution. I'm willing to do what I can in other ways."

Sarah said suspiciously: "What other ways?"

"Since you can't stick life at home, I'll do what I can to help you lead your own life somewhere else where you can be a good deal happier. Once Ann is my wife, I'm prepared to provide for her entirely. There will be plenty of money over for you. A nice little flat somewhere, that you can share with a girl friend. Furnish it and all that—just exactly as you want it."

Her eyes narrowed still more, Sarah said: "What a wonderfully generous man you are, Richard."

He suspected no sarcasm. Inwardly he was applauding himself. After all, the thing was quite simple. The girl knew perfectly well which side her bread was buttered. The whole thing was going to settle itself quite amicably.

He smiled at her good-humouredly.

"Well, I don't like seeing people unhappy. And I realise, which your mother doesn't, that young people always hanker after going their own way and being independent. You'll be far happier on your own than living a cat-and-dog life here."

"So that's your suggestion, is it?"

"It's a very good idea. Everyone satisfied."

Sarah laughed. Richard turned his head sharply.

"You won't get rid of me as easily as that," said Sarah.

"But—"

"I won't go, I tell you. I won't go—"

Neither of them heard Ann's latch-key in the front door. She pushed open the door to find them standing glaring at each other. Sarah was shaking all over and repeating hysterically:

"I won't go—I won't go—I won't go—"

"Sarah—"

They both turned sharply. Sarah ran to her mother.

"Darling, darling, you won't let him send me away, will you? To live in a flat with a girl friend. I *hate* girl friends. I don't want to be on my own. I want to stay with you. Don't send me away, Mother. Don't—don't."

Ann said quickly, soothingly:

"Of course not. It's all right, darling." To Richard she

said sharply: "What have you been saying to her?"

"Making a perfectly common-sense suggestion."

"He hates me, and he'll make you hate me."

Sarah was sobbing wildly now. She was a hysterical child. Ann said quickly and soothingly:

"No, no, Sarah, don't be absurd."

She made a sign to Richard and said: "We'll talk about it some other time."

"No, we won't." Richard stuck his chin out. "We'll talk about it here and now. We've got to get matters straight."

"Oh, please." Ann moved forward, her hand to her head. She sat down on the sofa.

"No good getting out of it by having a headache, Ann! The question is, do I come first with you or does Sarah?"

"That's not the question."

"I say it is! All this has got to be settled once for all. I can't stand much more."

The loud tones of Richard's voice went through Ann's head setting every twingeing nerve on fire in a flurry of pain. She had had a difficult committee meeting, had come home tired out, and now she felt that her life as at present lived was quite unendurable.

She said faintly: "I can't talk to you now, Richard. I really can't. I just can't stand any more."

"I tell you it's got to be settled. Either Sarah gets out of here, or I do."

A faint quiver ran through Sarah's body. She lifted her chin, staring at Richard.

"My plan's a perfectly sensible one," said Richard. "I've outlined it to Sarah. She didn't seem to have much against it until you came in."

"I won't go," said Sarah.

"My good girl, you can come and see your mother whenever you want to, can't you?"

Sarah turned passionately to Ann, flinging herself down beside her.

"Mother, Mother, you won't turn me out? You won't, will you? You're my mother."

A flush rose in Ann's face. She said with sudden firmness:

"I shall not ask my only daughter to leave her home unless she wants to do so."

Richard shouted: "She would want to—if it weren't to spite me."

"That's the sort of thing *you* would think!" Sarah spat at him.

"Hold your tongue," shouted Richard.

Ann raised her hands to her head.

"I can't bear this," she said, "I'm warning you both, I can't bear it . . ."

Sarah cried appealingly:

"Mother . . ."

Richard turned on Ann angrily:

"It's no use, Ann. You and your headaches! You've got to choose, damn it all."

"Mother," Sarah was really beside herself now. She clung to Ann like a frightened child. "Don't let him turn you against me. Mother . . . don't let him . . ."

Ann, her hands still clutching her head, said: "I can't bear any more. You'd better go, Richard."

"What?" He stared at her.

"Please go. Forget me . . . It's no use. . . ."

Again anger enveloped him. He said grimly:

"Do you realise what you're saying?"

Ann said distractedly: "I must have peace . . . I can't go on . . ."

Sarah whispered again: "Mother. . . ."

"Ann . . ." Richard's voice was full of incredulous pain.

Ann cried desperately: "It's no use . . . it's no *use*, Richard."

Sarah turned on him furiously and childishly:

"Go away," she said, "we don't want you, do you hear? We don't want you . . ."

There was a triumph in her face that would have been ugly if it had not been so childish.

He paid no attention to her. He was looking at Ann.

He said very quietly: "Do you mean this? I shan't—come back."

In an exhausted voice Ann said:

"I know . . . It just—can't be, Richard. Good-bye . . ."

He walked slowly out of the room.

Sarah cried: "Darling" and buried her head on her mother's lap.

Mechanically, Ann's hand stroked her daughter's head, but her eyes were on the door through which Richard had just gone out.

A moment later she heard the sound of the front door closing with a decisive bang.

She felt the same coldness she had felt that day at Victoria Station together with a great desolation. . . .

Richard was walking down the stairs now, out into the court-yard and away down the street. . . .

Walking out of her life. . . .

BOOK 2

Chapter one
1

Laura Whitstable looked affectionately through the windows of the Airway bus at the familiar streets of London. She had been away from London a long time, serving on a Royal Commission which had entailed an interesting and prolonged tour round the globe. The final sessions in the United States had been strenuous. Dame Laura had lectured and presided and lunched and dined, and had found difficulty in finding time to see her own personal friends.

Well, it was over now. She was home again, with a suit-case filled with notes and statistics and relevant papers, and with the prospect of a good deal more strenuous work ahead of her preparing for publication.

She was a woman of great vitality and enormous physical toughness. The prospect of work was always more alluring to her than the prospect of leisure, but unlike many people, she did not pride herself on the fact, and would sometimes disarmingly admit that the preference might be regarded as a weakness rather than a virtue. For work, she would say, was one of the chief avenues by which one escapes from oneself. And to live with oneself, without subterfuge, and in humility and content, was to attain the only true harmony of life.

Laura Whitstable was a woman who concentrated on one thing at a time. She had never been given to writing long newsy letters to friends. When she was absent, she was absent —in thought as well as in body.

She did conscientiously send highly-coloured picture

postcards to her domestic staff who would have been affronted if she had not done so. But her friends and intimates were aware that the first they would hear of Laura was a deep gruff voice on the telephone announcing that she was back again.

It was good to be home, Laura thought, a little later, as she looked round her comfortable mannish sitting-room and listened with half an ear to Bassett's melancholy unimpassioned catalogue of small domestic disasters that had occurred in her absence.

She dismissed Bassett with a final "Quite right to tell me" and sank into the large, shabby leather-covered armchair. Letters and periodicals were heaped on a side table, but she did not bother about them. Everything urgent had been dealt with by her efficient secretary.

She lit a cigar and leant back in the chair, her eyes half closed.

This was the end of one period, the beginning of another. . . .

She relaxed, letting the engine of her brain slow down and change over to the new rhythm. Her fellow commissioners—the problems that had arisen—speculations—points of view—American personalities—her American friends . . . gently, inexorably, they all receded, became shadowy . . .

London, the people she must see, the bigwigs whom she would bully, the Ministries to which she proposed to make herself a nuisance, the practical measures that she intended to take—the reports she must write . . . it all came clearly into her mind. The future campaign, the gruelling daily tasks. . . .

But before that there was an interregnum, a settling in again. Personal relationships and pleasures. Her own personal friends to see—a revived interest in their troubles and joys. A revisiting of her favourite haunts—all the hundred and one pleasures of her intimate private life. Presents that she had brought home with her to be bestowed. . . . Her rugged face softened and she smiled. Names floated into her mind. Charlotte—young David—Geraldine and her children—old Walter Emlyn—Ann and Sarah—Professor Parkes . . .

What had happened to them all since she had been away?

She would go down to see Geraldine in Sussex—the day after tomorrow if that was convenient. She reached out for the telephone, got through, fixed a day and a time. Then she rang old Professor Parkes. Blind and almost stone deaf, he nevertheless seemed to be in the best of health and spirits and eager for a real furious controversy with his old friend Laura.

The next number she rang was that of Ann Prentice.

It was Edith who answered.

"Well, this is a surprise, ma'am. A long time it's been. Read a piece about you in the paper, I did, not above a month or two ago. No, I'm sorry, Mrs. Prentice is out. Nearly always out in the evening she is, nowadays. Yes, Miss Sarah's out, too. Yes, ma'am, I'll tell Mrs. Prentice you rang and that you're back again."

Restraining a desire to remark that it would have been harder for her to ring up if she hadn't been back again, Laura Whitstable rang off, and proceeded to dial another number.

During the ensuing conversations and the making of arrangements to meet, Laura Whitstable relegated to the back of her mind some small point which she promised herself to examine later.

It was not until she was in bed that her analytical mind questioned why something that Edith had said had surprised her. It was a moment or two before it came back to her, but at last she pinned it down. Edith had said that Ann was out and that she nearly always was out in the evenings, nowadays.

Laura frowned because it seemed to her that Ann must have changed very much in her habits. Sarah, naturally, might be supposed to go racketing around every evening of her life. Girls did. But Ann was the quiet type—an occasional dinner engagement—a cinema now and then—or a play—but not a nightly routine.

Lying in bed Laura Whitstable thought about Ann Prentice for some time . . .

2

It was a fortnight later that Dame Laura rang the bell of Ann Prentice's flat.

Edith opened the door, and her sour face changed ever so slightly, indicating that she was pleased.

She stood aside as Dame Laura entered.

"Mrs. Prentice is just dressing to go out," she said. "But I know she'll want to see you."

She ushered Dame Laura into the sitting-room and her footsteps stumped along the passage towards Ann's bedroom.

Laura looked round the room in some surprise. It was completely transformed—she would hardly have known it for the same room, and just for a moment she toyed with the absurd idea that she had come to the wrong flat.

A few pieces of the original furniture remained, but across one corner was a big cocktail bar. The new *décor* was an up-to-date version of French Empire, with smartly striped satin curtains and a good deal of gilt and ormolu. The few pictures on the wall were modern. It looked less like a room in somebody's home, than like a "set" for a stage production.

Edith looked in to say:

"Mrs. Prentice will be with you in a moment, ma'am."

"This is a complete transformation scene," remarked Dame Laura, indicating her surroundings.

"Cost a mint of money, it did," said Edith with disapproval. "And one or two very odd young men there's been here seeing to it all. You wouldn't believe."

"Oh yes, I would," said Dame Laura. "Well, they seem to have made a very good job of it."

"Gimcrack," said Edith with a sniff.

"One must go with the times, Edith. I expect Miss Sarah likes it very much."

"Oh, it's not Miss Sarah's taste. Miss Sarah, she's never one for change. Never was. Why, you remember her, ma'am, didn't even like the sofa turned the other way! No, it's Mrs. Prentice that's so mad about all this."

Dame Laura raised her eyebrows slightly. It seemed to her again that Ann Prentice must have changed a good deal. But at that moment steps came hurrying down the passage, and Ann herself rushed in, her hands outstretched.

"Laura darling, how wonderful. I've been longing to see you."

She gave Laura a rapid and perfunctory kiss. The older woman studied her with surprise.

Yes, Ann Prentice had changed. Her hair, soft leaf-brown hair with a thread or two of grey, had been hennaed and cut in the latest and most extreme style. Her eyebrows had been plucked and her face was expensively made up. She was wearing a short cocktail dress adorned with a large and bizarre cluster of costume jewellery. Her movements were restless and artificial—and that, to Laura Whitstable, was the most significant change of all. For a gentle unhurried repose had been the chief characteristic of the Ann Prentice she had known two years ago.

Now she moved about the room, talking, fidgeting with small trifles and hardly waiting for an answer to what she said.

"It's such a long time—really ages—of course I've read about you occasionally in the paper. What was India like? They seem to have made a terrific fuss of you in the States? I suppose you had lovely food—beefsteaks—all that? And nylons! When did you get back?"

"A fortnight ago. I rang you up. You were out. I daresay Edith forgot to tell you."

"Poor old Edith. Her memory's not what it was. No, I think she did tell me, and I did mean to ring up—only you know what things are." She gave a little laugh. "One lives in such a rush."

"You usen't to live in a rush, Ann."

"Didn't I?" Ann was vague. "It seems impossible to avoid it. Have a drink, Laura. Gin and lime?"

"No, thanks. I never drink cocktails."

"Of course. Brandy and soda is your tipple. Here you are." She poured out the drink and brought it over, and then returned to get a drink for herself.

"How's Sarah?" asked Dame Laura.

Ann said vaguely:

"Oh, very well and gay. I hardly ever see her. Where's the gin? Edith! Edith!"

Edith came in.

"Why isn't there any gin?"

"Hasn't come," said Edith.

"I told you we must always have a reserve bottle. It's too sickening! You *must* see to it that we always have plenty of drink in the house."

"Enough comes in, goodness knows," said Edith. "A sight too much, to my way of thinking."

"That will do, Edith," cried Ann angrily. "Go round and get some."

"What, now?"

"Yes, now."

As Edith retreated, looking grim, Ann said angrily:

"She forgets everything. She's hopeless!"

"Well, don't work yourself up, my dear. Come and sit down and tell me all about yourself."

"There's nothing much to tell," Ann laughed.

"You're going out? Am I keeping you?"

"Oh no, no. My boy friend's coming to fetch me."

"Colonel Grant?" asked Dame Laura, smiling.

"Poor old James? Oh no. I hardly ever see him nowadays."

"How's that?"

"These old men are really so terribly boring. James is a dear, I know—but those long rambling stories of his . . . I just feel I can't stand it." Ann shrugged her shoulders. "Awful of me—but there it is!"

"You haven't told me about Sarah. Has she got a young man?"

"Oh, lots of them. She's very popular, thank goodness . . . I really couldn't face having a daughter who was all wet."

"Not any particular young man, then?"

"We-ell. It's hard to say. Girls never tell their mothers anything, do they?"

"What about young Gerald Lloyd—the one you were rather worried about?"

"Oh, he went off to South America or somewhere. That's all washed up, thank goodness. Fancy your remembering that!"

"I remember things about Sarah. I'm very fond of her."

"Sweet of you, Laura. Sarah's all right. Very selfish and tiresome in many ways—but I suppose that has to be at her age. She'll be in presently and then—"

The telephone rang and Ann broke off to answer it.

"Hullo? . . . Oh it's you, darling . . . Why, of course, I'd love to . . . Yes, but I'll have to look in my little book . . . Oh, bother, I don't know where it is . . . Yes, I'm sure it's all right . . . Thursday, then . . . the *Petit Chat* . . . Yes, wasn't it? . . . Funny the way Johnnie passed out completely . . . Well, of course, we were all a bit tight . . . Yes, I do agree . . ."

She replaced the receiver, remarking to Laura with a note of satisfaction in her voice that belied the words:

"That telephone! It goes all day long."

"It's a habit they have," Laura Whitstable agreed dryly. She added: "You seem to be leading a very gay life, Ann?"

"One can't vegetate, darling—oh, that sounds like Sarah."

Outside in the hall they heard Sarah's voice:

"Who? Dame Laura? Oh, splendid!"

She flung open the sitting-room door and came in. Laura Whitstable was struck by her beauty. The awkward touch of coltishness had gone, she was now a remarkably attractive young woman, with a quite unusual loveliness of face and form.

She looked radiant with pleasure at the sight of her god-mother and kissed her warmly.

"Laura darling, how lovely. You do look wonderful in that hat. Almost Royal with a weeny touch of the militant Tyrolean."

"Impertinent child," said Laura, smiling at her.

"No, but I mean it. You really are a Personage, aren't you, pet?"

"And you're a very handsome young woman!"

"Oh, that's just my expensive make-up."

The telephone rang and Sarah picked it up.

"Hullo? Who's speaking? Yes, she's here. It's for you, Mother—as usual."

As Ann took the receiver from her, Sarah sat on the arm of Laura's chair.

"The telephone rings for Mother all day long," she said, laughing.

Ann said sharply:

"Be quiet, Sarah, I can't hear. Yes . . . well, I think so . . . but next week I'm terribly booked up . . . I'll look in my little book." Turning, she said, "Sarah, find my book. It must be by my bed . . ." Sarah went out of the room. Ann went on talking into the telephone. "Well, of course I know what you mean . . . yes, that sort of thing is an awful bind . . . Do you, darling? . . . Well, as far as I'm concerned I've had Edward . . . I . . . oh, here's my book. Yes . . ." she took it from Sarah, turning the pages . . . "No, I can't manage Friday . . . Yes, I could go on afterwards . . . Very well then, we'll meet at the Lumley Smiths . . . Oh yes, I do agree. She's terribly wet."

She replaced the receiver and exclaimed:

"That telephone! I shall go off my head . . ."

"You adore it, Mother. And you adore gadding about, you know you do." Sarah turned to Dame Laura and demanded, "Don't you think Mother is looking awfully smart with that new hair-do? Years younger."

Ann said with a slightly artificial laugh:

"Sarah won't let me sink into graceful middle-age."

"Now, Mother, you know you like being gay. She's got far more boy friends than I have, Laura, and she's seldom home before dawn."

"Don't be absurd, Sarah," said Ann.

"Who is it tonight, Mother? Johnnie?"

"No, Basil."

"Oh, sooner you than me. I really think Basil is pretty well the end."

"Nonsense," said Ann sharply. "He's very amusing. What about you, Sarah? You're going out, I suppose?"

"Yes, Lawrence is coming for me. I must rush and change."

"Go on, then. And Sarah—*Sarah*—don't leave your things all over the place. Your fur—and your gloves. And pick up that glass. It will get broken."

"Oh all right, Mother, don't fuss."

"Someone has to fuss. You never clear up anything. Really, sometimes I don't know how I stand it! No—take them *with* you!"

As Sarah went out, Ann sighed in an exasperated fashion.

"Really, girls are absolutely maddening. You've no idea how trying Sarah is!"

Laura gave her friend a quick sideways glance.

There had been a note of real bad temper and irritation in Ann's voice.

"Don't you get tired with so much rushing about, Ann?"

"Of course I do—dead tired. Still, one must do something to amuse oneself."

"You never used to have much difficulty amusing yourself."

"Sit at home with a good book and have a meal on a tray? One goes through that dull period. But I've got my second wind now. By the way, Laura, it was you who first used that expression. Aren't you glad to see it's come true?"

"I didn't exactly mean the social round."

"Of course you didn't, darling. You meant take up some worthy object. But we can't all be public characters like you, tremendously scientific and serious-minded. I like being gay."

"What does Sarah like? Does she like being gay too? How is the child? Happy?"

"Of course. She has a wonderful time."

Ann spoke lightly and carelessly, but Laura Whitstable frowned. As Sarah had gone out of the room, Laura had been disturbed by a momentary expression of deep weariness on the girl's face. It was as though for a moment the smiling mask had slipped—underneath it Laura thought she had glimpsed uncertainty and something like pain.

Was Sarah happy? Ann evidently thought so. And Ann would know.

"Don't fancy things, woman," said Laura Whitstable to herself, sternly.

But in spite of herself she felt uneasy and disturbed. There was something not quite right in the atmosphere of the flat. Ann, Sarah, even Edith—all of them were conscious of it. All of them, she thought, had something to hide. Edith's grim look of disapproval, Ann's restlessness and nervous artificial manner, Sarah's brittle poise . . . There was something wrong somewhere.

The front door-bell rang and Edith, her face grimmer than ever, announced Mr. Mowbray.

Mr. Mowbray darted in. There was no other term for it. It was the skimming motion of some gay insect. Dame Laura thought that he would play Osric well. He was young and affected in manner.

"Ann!" he exclaimed. "So you're wearing it! My dear, it's the greatest success."

He held off, his head on one side, studying Ann's dress, while Ann introduced him to Dame Laura.

He advanced upon her exclaiming with excitement:

"A cameo brooch. How absolutely *adorable!* I adore cameos. I've got a thing about them!"

"Basil has a thing about all Victorian jewellery," said Ann.

"My dear, they had imagination. Those heavenly heavenly lockets. Two people's hair all worked into a curl and a weeping willow or an urn. They can't do that hair work nowadays. It's a lost art. And wax flowers—I'm crazy about wax flowers —and little papier mâché tables. Ann, you must let me take you to see a really divine table. Fitted up inside with the original tea caddies. Wickedly wickedly expensive, but it's worth it."

Laura Whitstable said:

"I must be going. Don't let me keep you."

"Stay and talk to Sarah," said Ann. "You've hardly seen her. And Lawrence Steene won't be calling for her yet awhile."

"Steene? Lawrence Steene?" Dame Laura asked sharply.

"Yes, Sir Harry Steene's son. Most attractive."

"Oh, do you think so, darling?" said Basil. "He always seems to me rather *melodramatic*—a little like a bad film. But women all seem to go quite crazy about him."

"He's disgustingly rich," said Ann.

"Yes, there's that. Most rich people are so deadly unattractive. It hardly seems fair that anyone should have money and attraction."

"Well, I suppose we'd better go," said Ann. "I'll ring you up, Laura, and we'll arrange for a lovely long talk sometime."

She kissed Laura in a faintly artificial manner and she and Basil Mowbray went out.

In the hall Dame Laura heard Basil say: "What a wonderful Period Piece she is—so divinely grim. Why have I never met her before?"

Sarah rushed in a few minutes later.

"Haven't I been quick? I hurried and hardly did anything to my face."

"That's a pretty frock, Sarah."

Sarah whirled round. She was wearing a pale eau-de-nil satin that clung to the lovely lines of her figure.

"Like it? It was wickedly expensive. Where's Mother? Gone off with Basil? He's pretty terrible, isn't he, but he's very amusing and spiteful and he makes a sort of special cult of older women."

"He probably finds it pays," said Dame Laura grimly.

"What an old cynic you are—and horribly right, too! But after all, Mother must have *some* fun. She's enjoying herself madly, poor pet. And she really is awfully attractive, don't you think so? Oh dear, it must be terrible to grow old!"

"It's quite comfortable, I can assure you," said Dame Laura.

"It's all very well for *you*—but we can't all be Personages! What have you been doing all these years since we've seen you?"

"Generally throwing my weight about. Interfering with other people's lives and telling them how easy and pleasant and well and happy they will be if they do exactly as I tell them. In fact, making a nuisance of myself in an overbearing way."

Sarah laughed affectionately.

"Will you tell me just how to manage my life?"

"Do you need telling?"

"Well, I'm not sure that I'm being very clever about it."

"Anything the matter?"

"Not really . . . I have a lovely time and all that. I suppose really I ought to *do* something."

"What sort of thing?"

Sarah said vaguely:

"Oh, I don't know. Take something up. Train for something. Archaeology or shorthand and typing, or massage, or architecture."

"What a wide range! No special bent?"

"No—no, I don't think so. . . . This flower job is all right, but I'm a bit sick of it. I don't know what I want really. . . ."

Sarah wandered aimlessly about the room.

"Not thinking of getting married?"

"Oh, marriage!" Sarah made an expressive grimace. "Marriages always seem to go wrong."

"Not invariably."

Sarah said: "Well, most of my friends seem to have come apart. It's all right for a year or two and then it goes wrong. Of course if you marry someone with pots of money, I suppose it's all right."

"So that's your view?"

"Well, it's really the only sensible one. Love's all right in a way, but after all," Sarah went on glibly, "it's only based on sexual attraction, and that can't last."

"You seem as well informed as a text-book," said Dame Laura dryly.

"Well, it's true, isn't it?"

"Perfectly true," Laura replied promptly.

Sarah looked faintly disappointed.

"Therefore the only sensible thing is to marry someone—really well off."

A faint smile twisted Laura Whitstable's lips.

"That mightn't last either," she said.

"Yes, I suppose money is a bit uncertain these days."

"I didn't mean that," said Dame Laura. "I meant that the pleasure of having money to spend is like sexual attraction. One gets used to it. It wears off like everything else."

"It wouldn't with me," said Sarah positively. "Really lovely clothes . . . and furs—and jewellery—and a yacht—"

"What a child you are still, Sarah."

"Oh, but I'm not, Laura. I feel very old and disillusioned sometimes."

"Do you?" Dame Laura could not help smiling a little at Sarah's young and beautiful earnest face.

"I think really I ought to get out of here somehow," said Sarah unexpectedly. "Take a job or get married, or something. I get on Mother's nerves frightfully. I try to be nice, but it doesn't seem to work. Of course, I am difficult, I suppose. Life is odd, isn't it, Laura? One moment everything is such fun and you're enjoying yourself, and then it all seems to go wrong, and you don't know where you are and what you want to do. And there isn't anyone you can talk to. And sometimes I get a funny feeling of being scared. I don't know why or what of. . . . But just—*scared*. Perhaps I ought to be analysed or something."

The front door-bell sounded. Sarah jumped up.

"That's Lawrence, I expect!"

"Lawrence Steene?" Laura asked sharply.

"Yes. Do you know him?"

"I've heard about him," said Laura. Her tone was rather grim.

Sarah laughed.

"No good, I'll be bound," she said, as Edith opened the door and announced: "Mr. Steene."

Lawrence Steene was tall and dark. He was about forty and looked it. He had rather curious eyes, almost veiled by the lids, and a languorous animal-like grace of movement.

He was the sort of man of whom women are immediately conscious.

"Hullo, Lawrence," said Sarah. "This is Lawrence Steene. My godmother, Dame Laura Whitstable."

Lawrence Steene came across and took Dame Laura's hand. He bowed over it in a manner that was slightly theatrical and might almost have been impertinent.

"This is indeed an honour," he said.

"You see, darling?" said Sarah. "You really *are* Royalty! It must be great fun to be a Dame. Do you think I shall ever be one?"

"I should think it most unlikely," said Lawrence.

"Oh, why?"

"Your talents lie in other directions."

He turned to Dame Laura.

"I was reading an article of yours only yesterday. In the *Commentator*."

"Oh yes," said Dame Laura. "On the stability of marriage."

Lawrence murmured:

"You seemed to take it for granted that stability in marriage was to be desired. But to my mind it is the impermanence of marriage nowadays which constitutes its greatest charm."

"Lawrence has been married a good deal," put in Sarah mischievously.

"Only three times, Sarah."

"Dear me," said Dame Laura. "Not another case of brides in the bath, I hope?"

"He sheds them in the divorce court," said Sarah. "Much simpler than death."

"But regrettably more expensive," said Lawrence.

"I believe I knew your second wife when she was a girl," said Laura. "Moira Denham, am I right?"

"Yes, indeed."

"A very charming girl."

"I do agree with you. She was quite delightful. So unsophisticated."

"A quality for which one sometimes pays heavily," said Laura Whitstable.

She got up.

"I must go."

"We can drop you," said Sarah.

"No, thanks. I feel like a brisk walk. Good-night, my dear."

The door shut briskly behind her.

"The disapproval," said Lawrence, "was marked. I'm a bad influence in your life, Sarah. The dragon Edith positively breathes fire from her nostrils whenever she lets me in."

"Hush," said Sarah. "She'll hear you."

"That's the worst of flats. No privacy . . ."

He had moved very close to her. Sarah moved away a little, saying flippantly:

"No, nothing's private in a flat, not even the plumbing."

"Where's your mother this evening?"

"She's out to dinner."

"Your mother is one of the wisest women I know."

"In what way?"

"She never interferes, does she?"

"No—oh no . . ."

"As I said—a wise woman. . . . Well, let's go." He stood back a minute looking at her. "You look your best tonight, Sarah. That's as it should be."

"Why all this fuss about tonight? Is it a special occasion?"

"It's a celebration. I'll tell you what we're celebrating later."

Chapter two

It was some hours later when Sarah repeated her question.

They were sitting in the hazy atmosphere of one of London's most expensive night-clubs. It was crowded, insufficiently ventilated and, as far as could be seen, had nothing about it to distinguish it from any other night-club, nevertheless it was, just for the time being, the fashion.

Once or twice Sarah had tried to approach the subject of

what they were celebrating, but Steene had successfully parried her attempts. He was an adept in producing the right sense of heightened interest.

As she smoked and looked round her, Sarah said: "Lots of Mother's stuffy old friends think it's terrible that I'm allowed to come to this place."

"And still worse that you're allowed to come here with me?"

Sarah laughed.

"Why are you supposed to be so dangerous, Larry? Do you go about seducing innocent young girls?"

Lawrence shuddered affectedly and said: "Nothing so crude."

"What, then?"

"I'm supposed to participate in what newspapers call nameless orgies."

Sarah said frankly: "I've heard that you do have rather peculiar parties."

"Some people would call them that. The simple truth is that I'm not conventional. There's so much to be done with life if you've only got the courage to experiment."

Sarah kindled eagerly.

"That's what *I* think."

Steene went on:

"I don't really care about young girls much. Silly fluffy crude little things. But you're different, Sarah. You've got courage and fire—real fire in you." His eyes drifted meaningly over her in a slow caress. "You've got a beautiful body, too. A body that can enjoy sensation—can taste—can feel. . . . You hardly know your own potentialities yet."

With an effort to hide her inner reaction, Sarah said lightly:

"You've got a very good line there, Larry. I'm sure it always goes down well."

"My dear—most girls bore me to distraction. You—don't. Hence—" he raised his glass to her—"our celebration."

"Yes—but what are we celebrating? Why all the mystery?"

He smiled at her.

"No mystery. It's quite simple. My divorce decree was made absolute today."

"Oh—" Sarah looked startled. Steene was watching her. "Yes, it clears the way. Well—what about it, Sarah?"

"What about what?" said Sarah.

Steene spoke with a sudden telling savagery:

"Don't play the wide-eyed innocent with me, Sarah. You know well enough I—want you. You've known it for some time."

Sarah avoided his glance. Her heart was beating pleasurably. There was something very exciting about Larry.

"You find most women attractive, don't you?" she asked lightly.

"Only a very few nowadays. At the moment—only you." He paused and then said quietly and almost casually: "You're going to marry me, Sarah."

"I don't want to get married. Anyway, I should think you'd be glad to be free again without tying yourself up immediately."

"Freedom is an illusion."

"You're not a very good advertisement for matrimony. Your last wife was pretty unhappy, wasn't she?"

Lawrence said calmly:

"She cried almost incessantly for the last two months we were together."

"Because, I suppose, she cared for you?"

"So it seemed. She was always an incredibly stupid woman."

"Why did you marry her?"

"She was so exactly like an early Primitive Madonna. My favourite period of art. But that sort of thing palls on one in the home."

"You're a cruel devil, aren't you, Larry?" Sarah was half revolted, half fascinated.

"That's really what you like about me. If I were the type of man to make you a good, steady and faithful husband you wouldn't think twice about me."

"Well, you're frank, at any rate."

"Do you want to live tamely, Sarah, or dangerously?"

Sarah did not answer. She pushed a small piece of bread round her side-plate. Then she said: "Your second wife—Moira Denham—the one Dame Laura knew—what—what about her?"

"You'd better ask Dame Laura." He smiled. "She'll give you chapter and verse. A sweet unsophisticated girl—and I broke her heart—putting it in the romantic vernacular."

"You seem a bit of a menace to wives, I must say."

"I didn't break my first wife's heart, I can assure you. Moral disapprobation was her reason for leaving me. A woman with a high standard. The truth of it is, Sarah, that women are never content to marry you for what you are. They wish you to be different. But at least you will admit that I do not conceal my real character from you. I like living dangerously, I like tasting forbidden pleasures. I have no high moral standards and I do not pretend to be what I am not."

He dropped his voice.

"I can give you a great deal, Sarah. I don't mean only what money can buy—furs to wrap round your adorable body, and jewels to put against your white skin. I mean that I can offer you the whole gamut of sensation. I can make you live, Sarah—I can make you *feel*. All life is experience, remember."

"I—yes, I suppose it is."

She was looking at him, half revolted, half fascinated. He leaned nearer to her.

"What do you really know of life, Sarah? Less than nothing! I can take you places, horrible sordid places, where you'll see life running fierce and dark, where you can feel—*feel*—till being alive is a dark ecstasy!"

He narrowed his eyes, watching the effect on her of his words. Then, deliberately, he broke the spell.

"Well," he said cheerfully, "we'd better get out of here."

He motioned the waiter to bring his bill.

Then he smiled at Sarah in a detached manner.

"Now I'm going to take you home."

In the luxurious darkness of the car, Sarah held herself taut and on the defensive, but Lawrence did not even attempt to touch her. Secretly she knew that she was disappointed. Smiling to himself, Lawrence was aware of that disappointment. Technically he knew a great deal about women.

He went up with her to the flat. Sarah opened the door with her key. She went into the sitting-room, switching on the light.

"A drink, Larry?"

"No, thanks. Good-night, Sarah."

She was impelled to call him back. He had counted on that.

"Larry."

"Yes?"

He stood in the doorway, his head turned over his shoulder.

His eyes swept over her with a connoisseur's approval. Perfect—quite perfect. Yes, he had got to have her. His pulses quickened a little, but he showed nothing in his face.

"You know—I think—"

"Yes?"

He came back towards her. They both spoke in low voices, mindful of the fact that Sarah's mother and Edith were presumably asleep near-by.

Sarah spoke in a hurried voice.

"You see, the fact is, I'm not really in love with you, Larry."

"Aren't you?"

Something in his tone made her voice hurry on, stammering a little.

"No—not really. Not properly. I mean, if you were to lose all your money and—oh, go and run an orange farm or something somewhere, I shouldn't think twice of you again."

"That would be very sensible."

"But that does show I'm not in love with you."

"Nothing would bore me more than romantic devotion. I don't want *that* from you, Sarah."

"Then—what do you want—?"

It was an unwise question—but she wanted to ask it. She wanted to go on. She wanted to see what—

He was very close beside her. Now, suddenly, he bent and

kissed the nape of her neck. His hands went round her, holding her breasts.

She began to pull away—then yielded. Her breath came faster.

A moment later, he released her.

"When you say you don't feel anything for me, Sarah," he said softly, "you're a liar."

And with that, he left her.

Chapter three

Ann had returned home some three-quarters of an hour before Sarah. On letting herself in with her latch-key, she was annoyed to see Edith's head, bristling with old-fashioned curling-pins, poking out of her bedroom.

Of late, she had been finding Edith more and more irritating.

Edith said at once:

"Miss Sarah isn't in yet."

A kind of unspoken criticism behind Edith's observation annoyed Ann. She snapped back:

"Why should she be?"

"Out gallivanting to all hours—and only a young girl."

"Don't be absurd, Edith. Things aren't what they used to be when I was a young girl. Girls are brought up now to look after themselves."

"More's the pity," said Edith. "And come to grief as a result of it, likely as not."

"They came to grief in my girlhood, too," said Ann dryly. "They were unsuspecting and ignorant, and all the chaperonage in the world didn't stop them from making fools of themselves if they were that type of girl. Nowadays girls read everything, do anything and go anywhere."

"Ah," said Edith darkly. "An ounce of experience is worth a pound of book learning. Well, if you're satisfied, it's none of my business—but there's gentlemen and gentlemen, if you take my meaning, and I don't take much to the one she's out with tonight. It's one of his type that got my sister Nora's second into her bit of difficulty——and no good crying your eyes out afterwards when the harm's done."

Ann could not help smiling in spite of her irritation. Edith and her relations! Moreover the picture of the self-confident Sarah as a betrayed village maiden tickled her sense of humour.

She said: "Well, stop fussing and go to bed. Did you get that sleeping prescription made up for me today?"

Edith grunted.

"You'll find it by your bed. But starting off taking things to make you sleep won't do you no good. . . . Won't be able to sleep without them, that's the next thing you'll know. To say nothing of making you more nervy than you are already."

Ann turned on her furiously:

"Nervy? I'm not nervy."

Edith did not reply. She merely pulled down the corners of her mouth, and retired into her room with a long pronounced indrawn hiss of the breath.

Ann went on angrily into her own room.

Really, she thought, every day Edith gets more and more impossible. Why I put up with it I don't know.

Nervy? Of course she wasn't nervy. Lately she'd formed the habit of lying awake——that was all. Everyone suffered from insomnia at some time or another. Much more sensible to take some stuff and give yourself a good night's rest, than lie awake hearing the clocks strike with your thoughts going round and round like——like squirrels in a cage. Dr. McQueen had been quite understanding about it and had given her a prescription——something quite mild and innocuous——bromide, she believed it was. Something to calm you down and stop you thinking. . . .

Oh dear, how tiresome everybody was. Edith and Sarah—— even dear old Laura. She felt a bit guilty about Laura. Of course she ought to have rung up Laura a week ago. Laura was one of her oldest friends. Only somehow, she hadn't wanted to be bothered with Laura——not just yet——Laura was sometimes rather difficult. . . .

Sarah and Lawrence Steene? Was there really anything in

it? Girls always liked going about with a man who had a bad reputation. . . . It probably wasn't serious. And even if it was . . .

Calmed by bromide, Ann fell asleep, but even in sleep she twitched and tossed restlessly on her pillows.

The telephone by her bed rang as she was sitting up drinking her coffee the following morning. Lifting the receiver, she was annoyed to hear the gruff tones of Laura Whitstable.

"Ann, does Sarah go out much with Lawrence Steene?"

"Good gracious, Laura, do you have to ring up at this hour in the morning to ask me that? How should I know?"

"Well, you are the girl's mother, aren't you?"

"Yes, but one doesn't catechise one's children the whole time asking where they go and with whom. They wouldn't stand for it, to begin with."

"Come now, Ann, don't fence with me. He's after her, isn't he?"

"Oh, I shouldn't think so. His divorce hasn't gone through yet, I imagine."

"The decree was made absolute yesterday. I saw it in the paper. How much do you know about him?"

"He's old Sir Harry Steene's only son. Rolling in money."

"And with a notorious reputation?"

"Oh, that! Girls are always attracted by a man with a bad reputation—that's been so ever since the time of Lord Byron. But it doesn't really mean anything."

"I'd like to have a talk with you, Ann. Will you be in this evening?"

Ann said quickly:

"No, I'm going out."

"About six, then."

"Sorry, Laura, I'm going to a cocktail party. . . ."

"Very well, then, I shall come about five—or would you—" Laura Whitstable's voice held grim determination— "prefer that I came round *now?*"

Ann capitulated gracefully.

"Five o'clock—that will be lovely."

She replaced the receiver with a sigh of exasperation.

Really, Laura was impossible! All these Commissions, and Unescos and Unos—they turned women's heads.

"I don't want Laura coming here all the time," said Ann to herself fretfully.

Nevertheless she received her friend with every sign of pleasure when the latter made her appearance. She chattered gaily and nervously while Edith brought in tea. Laura Whitstable was unusually unassertive. She listened and responded, but that was all.

Then, with conversation petered out, Dame Laura put down her cup and said with her usual forthrightness:

"I'm sorry to worry you, Ann, but as it happened, coming back from the States I heard two men discussing Larry Steene—and what they said wasn't particularly pleasant hearing."

Ann gave a quick shrug of her shoulders.

"Oh, the things one overhears—"

"Are often intensely interesting," said Dame Laura. "They were quite decent men—and their opinion of Steene was pretty damning. Then there's Moira Denham who was his second wife. I knew her before she married him and I knew her afterwards. She was a complete nervous wreck."

"Are you suggesting that Sarah—"

"I'm not suggesting that Sarah would be reduced to a nervous wreck if she married Lawrence Steene. She has a more resilient nature. Nothing of the butterfly on the wheel about Sarah."

"Well, then—"

"But I do think she might be very unhappy. And there's one third point. Did you read in the papers about a young woman called Sheila Vaughan Wright?"

"Something to do with being a drug addict?"

"Yes. It's the second time she's been up in court. She was a friend of Lawrence Steene's at one time. All I'm saying to you, Ann, is that Lawrence Steene is a particularly nasty bit of goods—in case you don't know it already—but perhaps you do?"

"I know there's talk about him, of course," said Ann rather

reluctantly. "But what do you expect me to do about it? I can't forbid Sarah to go out with him. If I did, it would probably drive her the other way. Girls won't stand being dictated to, as you know very well. It would simply make the whole thing more important. As it is, I don't suppose for a minute there's anything serious in it. He admires her and she's flattered because he's said to be a bad lot. But you seem to be assuming that he wants to marry her—"

"Yes, I think he wants to marry her. He's what I would describe as a Collector."

"I don't know what you mean."

"It's a type—and not the best type. Supposing she does want to marry him. How would you feel about it?"

Ann said bitterly: "What would be the good of my feeling anything? Girls do exactly as they like and marry whom they please."

"But Sarah is very much influenced by you."

"Oh, no, Laura, you're wrong there. Sarah goes her own way entirely. I don't interfere."

Laura Whitstable stared at her.

"You know, Ann, I can't quite make you out. Wouldn't you be upset if she married this man?"

Ann lit a cigarette and puffed at it impatiently.

"It's all so difficult. Lots of men with bad reputations have made quite good husbands—once they've sown their wild oats. Looking at it in the purely worldly sense, Lawrence Steene is a very good match."

"That wouldn't influence you, Ann. It's Sarah's happiness you want, not her material property."

"Oh, of course. But Sarah, in case you haven't realised it, is very fond of pretty things. She likes luxurious living—far more than I do."

"But she wouldn't marry solely on that account?"

"I don't think so." Ann sounded doubtful. "Actually, I think she is definitely attracted by Lawrence."

"And you think money might tip the scales?"

"I don't *know*, I tell you! I think that Sarah would—well—hesitate before she married a poor man. Let's put it like that."

"I wonder," said Dame Laura thoughtfully.

"Girls nowadays seem to think and talk of nothing but money."

"Oh, *talk!* I've heard Sarah talk, bless her. All very reasonable and hard-boiled and unsentimental. But language is given you to conceal your thoughts as much as to express them. Whatever generation it is, young women talk to pattern. The question is, what does Sarah really *want?*"

"I've no idea," said Ann. "I rather imagine—just a good time."

Dame Laura shot her a quick glance.

"You think she's happy?"

"Oh, yes. Really, Laura, she has a wonderful time."

Laura said meditatively:

"I didn't think she looked quite happy."

Ann said sharply:

"All these girls look discontented. It's a pose."

"Perhaps. So you don't feel you can do anything about Lawrence Steene?"

"I don't see what I can do. Why don't *you* talk to her about it?"

"I shan't do that. I'm only her godmother. I know my place."

Ann flushed angrily.

"I suppose you think it's *my* place to talk to her?"

"Not at all. As you say, talking doesn't do much good."

"But you think I ought to do something?"

"No, not necessarily."

"Then what do you mean?"

Laura Whitstable looked thoughtfully across the room.

"I only wondered what was going on in your mind."

"In *my* mind?"

"Yes."

"Nothing's going on in my mind. Nothing at all."

Laura Whitstable withdrew her glance from the other side of the room and gave Ann a quick bird-like glance.

"No," she said. "That's what I was afraid of."

"I don't understand you in the least."

Laura Whitstable said:

"What's going on isn't in your mind. It's farther down."

"Oh, if you're going to talk nonsense about the subconscious! Really, Laura, you—you seem to be accusing me in some way."

"*I'm* not accusing you."

Ann got up and began to pace up and down the room.

"I simply don't know what you mean. . . . I'm devoted to Sarah. . . . You know how much she's always meant to me. I—why, I've given up everything for her sake!"

Laura said gravely: "I know that you made a big sacrifice for her two years ago."

"Well?" demanded Ann. "Doesn't that show you?"

"Show me what?"

"How absolutely devoted I am to Sarah."

"My dear, it wasn't I who suggested that you weren't! You're defending yourself—but not against any accusation of mine." Laura got up. "I must go now. I may have been unwise to come—"

Ann followed her towards the door.

"You see, it's all so vague—nothing one can take hold of—"

"Yes, yes."

Laura paused. She spoke with a sudden startling energy.

"The trouble with a sacrifice is that it's not over and done with once it's made! It goes on. . . ."

Ann stared at her in surprise.

"What do you mean, Laura?"

"Nothing. Bless you, my dear, and take a word of advice from me—in my professional capacity. Don't live at such a pace that you haven't time to think."

Ann laughed, her good temper restored.

"I shall sit down and think when I'm too old to do anything else," she said gaily.

Edith came in to clear away and Ann, with a glance at the clock, uttered an exclamation and went to her bedroom.

She painted her face with special care, peering closely in the glass. The new hair-cut was, she thought, a success. It certainly made her look much younger. Hearing a knock at the front door, she called out to Edith:

"Any post?"

There was a pause as Edith examined the letters, then she said:

"Nothing but bills, ma'am—and one for Miss Sarah—from South Africa."

Edith put a slight stress on the last three words, but Ann did not notice. She returned to the sitting-room just as Sarah entered with her latch-key.

"What I hate about chrysanthemums is their beastly smell," Sarah grumbled. "I shall chuck Noreen and take a job as a mannequin. Sandra's dying to have me. It's better pay, too. Hullo, have you been having a tea party?" she asked, as Edith came in and gathered up a stray cup.

"Laura's been here."

"Laura? Again? She was here yesterday."

"I know." Ann hesitated a minute, then said: "She came to say that I oughtn't to let you go out with Larry Steene."

"Laura did? How very protective of her. Is she afraid I'll be eaten by a big bad wolf?"

"Apparently." Ann said deliberately: "It seems he has a very unsavoury reputation."

"Well, everyone knows *that!* Did I see some letters in the hall?" Sarah went out and returned holding a letter with a South African stamp.

Ann said:

"Laura seems to think that I ought to put a stop to it."

Sarah was staring down at the letter. She said absently: "What?"

"Laura thinks I ought to put a stop to you and Lawrence going out together."

Sarah said cheerfully:

"Darling, what could you do?"

"That's what I told her," said Ann triumphantly. "Mothers are quite helpless nowadays."

Sarah sat down on the arm of a chair and opened her letter. She spread out the two pages and began to read.

Ann went on:

"One really forgets that Laura is the age she is! She's getting so old that she's really completely out of touch with modern ideas. Of course, to be honest, I *have* been rather worried about your going out with Larry Steene so much—but I decided that if I said anything to you, it would make it much worse. I know that I can trust you not to do anything really foolish—"

She paused. Sarah, intent on her letter, murmured:

"Of course, darling."

"But you must feel free to choose your own friends. I do think that sometimes a lot of friction arises because—"

The telephone rang.

"Oh dear, that telephone!" cried Ann. She moved gladly across to it, and picked up the receiver expectantly.

"Hullo. . . . Yes, Mrs. Prentice speaking. . . . Yes. . . . Who? I can't quite catch the name . . . Cornford, did you say? . . . Oh, C—A—U—L—D . . . Oh! . . . *Oh!* . . . how stupid of me. . . . Is it you, Richard? . . . Yes, such a long time. . . . Well, that's very sweet of you. . . . No, of course not. . . . No, I'm delighted. . . . Really, I mean it. . . . I've often wondered . . . What have you been doing with yourself? . . . What? . . . Really? . . . I'm so glad. My best congratulations. . . . I'm sure she's charming. . . . That's very nice of you . . . I should love to meet her. . . ."

Sarah got up from the arm of the chair where she had been sitting. She went slowly towards the door, her eyes blank and unseeing. The letter she had been reading was crushed up in her hand.

Ann continued: "No, I couldn't tomorrow—no—just wait a moment. I'll get my little book. . . ." She called urgently: "Sarah!"

Sarah turned in the doorway.

"Yes?"

"Where's my little book?"

"Your book? I've no idea."

Sarah was miles away. Ann said irritably:

"Well, do look for it. It must be somewhere. Beside my bed, perhaps. Darling, do *hurry.*"

Sarah went out of the room and returned a moment later with Ann's engagement book.

"Here you are, Mother."

Ann ruffled its pages.

"Are you there, Richard? No, lunch isn't any good. I suppose you couldn't come round for drinks on Thursday? . . . Oh, I see. I'm sorry. And lunch no good either? . . . Well, *must* you go by a morning train? . . . Where are you staying? . . . Oh, but that's just round the corner. I know, can't you both come round straight away and have a quick drink? . . . No, I was going out—but I've heaps of time. . . . That will be delightful. Come right away."

She replaced the receiver and stood absent-mindedly staring into space.

Sarah said without much interest: "Who was that?" Then she added with an effort: "Mother. I've heard from Gerry. . . ."

Ann roused herself suddenly.

"Tell Edith to bring the best glasses in and some ice. Quickly. They're coming round for a drink."

Sarah moved obediently.

"Who is?" she asked, still without much interest.

Ann said: "Richard—Richard Cauldfield!"

"Who's he?" asked Sarah.

Ann looked at her sharply, but Sarah's face was quite blank. She went and called to Edith. When she returned Ann said with emphasis:

"It was Richard Cauldfield."

"Who's Richard Cauldfield?" Sarah looked puzzled.

Ann pressed her hands together. Her anger was so intense that she had to pause a minute to steady her voice.

"So—you don't even remember his name?"

Sarah's eyes had gone once more to the letter she was holding. She said quite naturally: "Did I know him? Tell me something about him."

Ann's voice was hoarse as she said, this time with a biting emphasis that could not be missed:

"*Richard Cauldfield.*"

Sarah looked up startled. Suddenly comprehension came to her.

"What! Not Cauliflower?"

"Yes."

To Sarah it was a huge joke.

"Fancy his turning up again," she said cheerfully. "Is he still after you, Mother?"

Ann said shortly: "No, he's married."

"That's a good job," said Sarah. "I wonder what she's like?"

"He's bringing her here for a drink. They'll be here almost at once. They're at the Langport. Tidy up these books, Sarah. Put your things in the hall. And your gloves."

Opening her bag, Ann surveyed her face anxiously in the small mirror. As Sarah returned she said:

"Do I look all right?"

"Yes, lovely." Sarah's reply was perfunctory.

She was frowning to herself. Ann shut her bag and moved restlessly about the room, altering the position of a chair, rearranging a cushion.

"Mother, I've heard from Gerry."

"Have you?"

The vase of bronze chrysanthemums would look better on the corner table.

"He's had awfully bad luck."

"Has he?"

The cigarette box here, and the matches.

"Yes, some sort of disease or something got into the oranges and then he and his partner got into debt and—and now they've had to sell up. The whole thing's a wash-out."

"What a pity. But I can't say I'm surprised."

"Why?"

"Something like that always seems to happen to Gerry," said Ann vaguely.

"Yes—yes, it does." Sarah was cast down. The generous indignation on Gerry's behalf was not so spontaneous now as it had been. She said half-heartedly: "It isn't his fault. . . ." But she was no longer as convinced as she would once have been.

"Perhaps not." Ann spoke absently. "But I'm afraid he'll always make a nonsense of things."

"Are you?" Sarah sat down again on the arm of her chair.

She said earnestly: "Mother, do you think—really—that Gerry never will get anywhere?"

"It doesn't look like it."

"And yet I know—I'm sure—there's a lot in Gerry."

"He's a charming boy," said Ann. "But I'm afraid he's one of the world's misfits."

"Perhaps," Sarah sighed.

"Where's the sherry? Richard always used to prefer sherry to gin. Oh, there it is."

Sarah said: "Gerry says he's going to Kenya—he and another pal of his. They're going to sell cars—and run a garage."

"It's extraordinary," commented Ann, "how many inefficients always end up running a garage."

"But Gerry was always a wizard with cars. He made that one he bought for ten pounds go wonderfully. And you know, Mother, it isn't that Gerry is really lazy or won't work. He does work—sometimes awfully hard. It's just, I think," she puzzled it out, "that his judgment's not very good."

For the first time, Ann gave her daughter her full attention. She spoke kindly but decisively.

"You know, Sarah, if I were you, I should—well, put Gerry right out of your mind."

Sarah looked shaken. Her lips quivered.

"Would you?" she asked uncertainly.

The electric bell rang, an insistent soulless summons.

"Here they are," said Ann.

She went and stood in a rather artificial attitude by the mantelpiece.

Chapter four

Richard came into the room with that little extra air of confidence that he always assumed when he was embarrassed.

If it hadn't been for Doris he wouldn't be doing this. But Doris had been curious. She'd gone on at him, pestered him, pouted, sulked. She was very pretty and young and, having married a man a good deal older than herself, she fully intended to see that she got her own way.

Ann came forward to meet them, smiling charmingly. She felt like someone playing a part on the stage.

"Richard—how nice to see you! And this is your wife?"

Behind the cover of polite greetings and nondescript remarks thoughts were busy.

Richard thought to himself:

"How she's changed . . . I'd hardly have known her. . . ."

And a kind of relief came to him as he thought:

"She wouldn't have done for me—not really. Too smart altogether . . . Fashionable. The gay kind. Not my sort."

And he felt a renewed affection for his wife, Doris. He was inclined to be besotted about Doris—she was so young. But there were times when he realised uneasily that that careful accent of hers was inclined to get on his nerves, and her continual archness was also a bit wearing. He did not admit that he had married out of his class—he had met her at a hotel on the south coast, and her people had plenty of money, her father was a retired builder—but there were times when her parents jarred on him. But less now than they had done a year ago. And he was coming to accept Doris's friends as the friends they would naturally make. It was not, as he knew, what he had once wanted . . . Doris would never take the place of his long dead Aline. But she had given him a second spring of the senses and for the moment that was enough.

Doris, who had been suspicious about this Mrs. Prentice and inclined to be jealous, was favourably surprised by Ann's appearance.

"Why, she's ever so old," she thought to herself with the cruel intolerance of youth.

She was impressed with the room and the furnishings. The daughter, too, was awfully smart and really looked quite like something in *Vogue*. She was a little impressed that her

Richard had once been engaged to this fashionable woman. It raised him in her estimation.

To Ann, the sight of Richard had come as a shock. This man who was talking so confidently to her was a stranger. Not only was he a stranger to her, she was a stranger to him. They had moved, he and she, in opposite directions and there was now between them no common meeting ground. She had always been conscious of Richard of dual tendencies. There had always been a strain of pompousness there, the tendency to a closed mind. He had been a simple man with interesting possibilities. The door had been shut on those possibilities. The Richard Ann had loved was imprisoned inside this good-humoured, slightly pompous, commonplace British husband.

He had met and married this common predatory child, with no qualities of heart and brain, only an assured pink and white prettiness and a youthful crude sex appeal.

He had married this girl because she, Ann, had sent him away. Smarting with anger and resentment, he had fallen an easy prey to the first female creature who had laid herself out to attract him. Well, perhaps it was all for the best. She supposed he was happy. . . .

Sarah brought them drinks and talked politely. Her thoughts were quite uncomplicated, represented entirely by the phrase: "What a crashing bore these people are!" She was aware of no undercurrents. At the back of her mind was still a dull ache connected with the word "Gerry."

"You've had all this done up, I see?"

Richard was looking round.

"It's lovely, Mrs. Prentice," said Doris. "All this Regency is the latest thing, isn't it? What was it before?"

"Old-fashioned rosy things," said Richard vaguely. He had a memory of the soft firelight and Ann and himself sitting on the old sofa that had been banished to make way for the Empire couch. "I liked them better than this."

"Men are such frightful sticks-in-the-mud, aren't they, Mrs. Prentice?" simpered Doris.

"My wife is determined to keep me up-to-date," said Richard.

"Of course I am, darling. I'm not going to let you turn into an old fogey before your time," said Doris affectionately. "Don't you think he looks years younger than when you saw him last, Mrs. Prentice?"

Ann avoided Richard's eye. She said:

"I think he looks splendid."

"I've taken up golf," said Richard.

"We've found a house near Basing Heath. Isn't it lucky? Quite a good train service for Richard to go up and down every day. And it's such a wonderful golf course. Very crowded, of course, at week-ends."

"It's enormous luck nowadays to get the house you're looking for," said Ann.

"Yes. It's got an Aga cooker and all wired for power and absolutely newly built on the latest lines. Richard hankered after one of these terrible old falling down decayed period houses. But I put my foot down! We woman are the practical ones, aren't we?"

Ann said politely:

"I'm sure a modern house saves a lot of domestic bother these days. Have you got a garden?"

Richard said: "Not really," just as Doris said: "Oh, *yes*."

His wife looked at Richard reproachfully.

"How can you say that, darling, after all the bulbs we've put in."

"Quarter of an acre round the house," said Richard.

For a moment his eyes met Ann's. They had talked together sometimes of the garden they would have if they went to live in the country. A walled garden for fruit—and a lawn with trees. . . .

Richard turned hastily to Sarah:

"Well, young woman, what do you do with yourself?" His old nervousness of her revived and made him sound peculiarly and odiously facetious. "Lots of wild parties, I suppose?"

Sarah laughed cheerfully, thinking to herself: "I'd forgotten how odious Cauliflower was. It's a good thing for Mother I settled his hash."

"Oh, yes," she said. "But I make it a rule not to end up in Vine Street more than twice a week."

"Girls drink far too much nowadays. Ruin their complexions—though I must say yours looks very good."

"You always were interested in cosmetics, I remember," said Sarah sweetly.

She crossed to Doris who was talking to Ann.

"Let me give you another drink."

"Oh, no, thanks, Miss Prentice—I couldn't. Even this has gone to my head. What a lovely cocktail bar you've got. It's all awfully smart, isn't it?"

"It's very convenient," said Ann.

"Not married yet, Sarah?" said Richard.

"Oh, no. I have hopes, though."

"I suppose you go to Ascot and all those sort of things," said Doris enviously.

"The rain this year ruined my best frock," said Sarah.

"You know, Mrs. Prentice," Doris turned again to Ann, "you're not a bit like what I imagined."

"What did you imagine?"

"But then men are so stupid at descriptions, aren't they?"

"How did Richard describe me?"

"Oh, I don't know. It wasn't exactly what he *said*. It was the impression I got. I pictured you somehow as one of those quiet mousy little women," she laughed shrilly.

"A quiet mousy little woman? How dreary that sounds!"

"Oh, no, Richard admired you *enormously*. He really *did*. Sometimes, you know, I've been quite *jealous*."

"That sounds most absurd."

"Oh, well, you know how one goes on. Sometimes when Richard is very quiet in the evening and won't talk I tease him by telling him he's thinking about you."

(Do you think of me, Richard? Do you? I don't believe you do. You try not to think of me—just as I try never to think of you.)

"If you're ever Basing Heath way, you *must* come and see us, Mrs. Prentice."

"That's very kind of you. I should love to."

"Of course, like everybody else, the domestic problem is our great trouble. Only dailies to be had—and so often unreliable."

Richard, turning away from his heavy-handed conversation with Sarah, said:

"You've still got your old Edith, I see, Ann?"

"Yes, indeed. We'd be lost without her."

"Jolly good cook she was. Very nice little dinners she used to turn out."

There was a moment's awkwardness.

One of Edith's little dinners—the firelight—the chintzes with their sprigs of rosebuds . . . Ann with her soft voice and her leaf-brown hair. . . . Talking—making plans . . . the happy future. . . . A daughter coming home from Switzerland—but he hadn't dreamt that *that* would ever matter. . . .

Ann was watching him. Just for a moment she saw the real Richard—her Richard—looking at her out of sad remembering eyes.

The real Richard? Wasn't Doris's Richard as real as Ann's Richard?

But now her Richard had gone again. It was Doris's Richard who was saying good-bye. More talk, more proffers of hospitality—would they never go? That nasty greedy little girl with her affected mincing voice. Poor Richard—Oh, poor Richard!—and it was her doing. She had sent him to that hotel lounge where Doris was waiting.

But was it really poor Richard? He had a young pretty wife. He was probably very happy.

At last! They had gone! Sarah, politely seeing them out, came back into the room, uttering a terrific "Whoof!"

"Thank goodness *that's* over! You know, Mother, you did have an escape."

"I suppose I did." Ann spoke like someone in a dream.

"Well, I ask you, would you like to marry him now?"

"No," said Ann. "I wouldn't like to marry him now."

(We've gone away from that meeting point there was in our lives. You've gone one way, Richard, and I've gone another. I'm not the woman who walked with you in St. James's Park, and you're not the man I was going to grow old with. . . . We're two different people—strangers. You didn't much care for the look of me today—and I found you dull and pompous. . . .)

"You'd be bored to death, you know you would," said Sarah's positive young voice.

"Yes," said Ann slowly. "It's quite true. I should be bored to death."

(I couldn't sit still now and drift on to old age. I must go out—be amused—things must happen.)

Sarah put a caressing hand on her mother's shoulder.

"No doubt about it, darling, what you really like is razzling. You'd be bored to death stuck in a suburb with a mingy little garden and nothin' to do but wait for Richard to come home on the 6.15, or tell you how he did the fourth hole in three! That's not your line of country at all."

"I should have liked it once."

(An old walled garden, and a lawn with trees, and a small Queen Anne house of rose-red bricks. And Richard would not have taken up golf, but would have sprayed rose trees and planted bluebells under the trees. Or if he had taken up golf, she would have been delighted he *had* done the fourth in three!)

Sarah kissed her mother's cheek affectionately.

"You ought to be very grateful to me, darling," she said, "for getting you out of it. If it hadn't been for me you'd have married him."

Ann drew away a little. Her eyes, the pupils distended, stared at Sarah.

"If it hadn't been for you, I should have married him. And now— I don't want to. He doesn't mean anything to me at all."

She walked to the mantlepiece, running her finger along it, her eyes dark with amazement and pain. She said softly:

"Nothing at all. . . . Nothing. . . . What a very bad joke life is!"

Sarah wandered over to the bar and poured herself out

another drink. She stood there, fidgeting a little, and finally, without turning round, she spoke in a rather would-be detached voice.

"Mother—I suppose I'd better tell you. Larry wants me to marry him."

"Lawrence Steene?"

"Yes."

There was a pause. Ann said nothing for some time. Then she asked:

"What are you going to do about it?"

Sarah turned. She shot a swift appealing glance at Ann, but Ann was not looking at her.

She said: "I don't know. . . ."

Her voice held a rather forlorn frightened note, like a child's. She looked hopefully at Ann, but Ann's face was hard and remote. Ann said after a moment or two:

"Well, it's for you to decide."

"I know."

From the table close to her, Sarah picked up Gerry's letter. She twisted it slowly in her fingers, staring down at it. At last she said with the sharpness almost of a cry:

"I don't know *what* to do!"

"I don't see how I can help you," said Ann.

"But what do you *think*, Mother? Oh, do say something."

"I've already told you that he hasn't got a good reputation."

"Oh *that!* That doesn't matter. I should be bored to death with a model of all the virtues."

"He's rolling in money, of course," said Ann. "He could give you a very good time. But if you don't care for him I shouldn't marry him."

"I do care for him in a way," said Sarah slowly.

Ann got up, looking at the clock.

"Well then," she said briskly, "what's the difficulty? My goodness, I forgot I was going to the Eliots. I shall be frightfully late."

"All the same, I'm not sure—" Sarah stopped. "You see—"

Ann said: "There's no one else is there?"

"Not really," said Sarah. Again she looked down at Gerry's letter twisted in her hand.

Ann said quickly:

"If you're thinking of Gerry, I should put him right out of your head, Sarah. Gerry's no good, and the sooner you make up your mind to that, the better."

"I suppose you're right," said Sarah slowly.

"I'm quite certain I'm right," said Ann briskly. "Wash Gerry right out. If you don't care for Lawrence Steene, don't marry him. You're very young still. There's plenty of time."

Sarah walked moodily over to the fireplace.

"I suppose I might as well marry Lawrence. . . . After all, he's madly attractive. Oh, mother," it was a sudden cry— "what *shall* I do?"

Ann said angrily:

"Really, Sarah, you behave exactly like a baby of two! How can I decide your life for you? The responsibility rests with you and you only."

"Oh, I know."

"Well, then?" Ann was impatient.

Sarah said childishly:

"I thought perhaps you could—help me somehow?"

Ann said: "I've already told you that there's no need for you to marry *anyone* unless you want to."

Still with that childish look on her face, Sarah said unexpectedly: "But you'd like to get rid of me, wouldn't you?"

Ann said sharply:

"Sarah, how can you say such a thing? Of course I don't want to get rid of you. What an idea!"

"I'm sorry, Mother. I didn't really mean that. Only it's all so different now, isn't it? I mean we used to have such fun together. But nowadays I always seem to be getting on your nerves."

"I'm afraid I am rather nervy sometimes," said Ann coldly. "But after all, you're rather temperamental yourself, aren't you, Sarah?"

"Oh, I daresay it's all my fault," Sarah went on reflectively: "Most of my friends are married. Pam and Betty and

Susan. Joan isn't but then she's gone all political." She paused again before going on. "It would really be rather fun to marry Lawrence. Glorious to have all the clothes and furs and things one wanted."

Ann said dryly: "I certainly think you'd better marry a man with money, Sarah. Your tastes are decidedly expensive. Your allowance is always overdrawn."

"I'd hate to be poor," said Sarah.

Ann took a deep breath. She felt insincere and artificial and she didn't quite know what to say.

"Darling, I don't really know how to advise you. You see, I do feel that this is so completely your own affair. It would be quite wrong for me to push you into it or to advise you against it. You *must* make up your mind for yourself. You do see that, Sarah, don't you?"

Sarah said quickly:

"Of course, darling—am I being a terrible bore?—I don't want to worry you. You might just tell me one thing. How do *you* feel about Lawrence?"

"I really haven't any feeling about him one way or the other."

"Sometimes—I feel just a bit—scared of him."

"Darling," Ann was amused, "isn't that rather silly?"

"Yes, I suppose it is . . ."

Slowly Sarah began to tear Gerry's letter, first in strips, then across and across. She threw the bits into the air and watched them float down like a snowstorm.

"Poor old Gerry," she said.

Then with a swift sideways glance she said:

"You do *mind* what happens to me, don't you, Mother?"

"Sarah! Really."

"Oh, I'm sorry—going on and on like this. I just feel awfully *queer* somehow. It's like being out in a snowstorm and not knowing which is the way home. . . . It's a frightfully queer feeling. Everything and everyone is different . . . . You're different, Mother."

"What absolute nonsense, pet, I really *must* go now."

"I suppose you must. Does this party matter?"

"Well, I want particularly to see the new murals Kit Eliot has had done."

"Oh, I see." Sarah paused and then said: "You know, Mother, I really think I may be much keener on Lawrence than I think I am."

"I shouldn't be surprised," said Ann lightly. "But don't be in a hurry. Good-bye, my sweet—I must fly."

The front door shut behind Ann.

Edith came out of the kitchen and into the sitting-room with a tray to clear away the glasses.

Sarah had put a record on the gramophone and was listening with a melancholy enjoyment to Paul Robeson singing "Sometimes I feel like a motherless child."

"The tunes you like!" said Edith. "Gives me the willies, that does."

"I think it's lovely."

"No accounting for tastes." Edith grunted crossly, as she observed: "Why can't people keep their cigarette ash in ash-trays. Flicking it all over the place."

"It's good for the carpet."

"That's always been said and it's no truer now than it ever was. And *why* you've got to scatter bits of paper all over the floor when the waste-paper basket's over by the wall—"

"Sorry, Edith. I didn't think. I was tearing up my past, and I wanted to make a gesture."

"Your past, indeed!" Edith snorted. Then she asked gently as she watched Sarah's face: "Anything wrong, my pretty?"

"Nothing at all. I'm thinking of getting married, Edith."

"No hurry for that. You wait until Mr. Right comes along."

"I don't believe it makes any difference who you marry. It's sure to go wrong anyway."

"Now don't you talk nonsense, Miss Sarah! What's all this about anyway?"

Sarah said wildly:

"I want to get away from here."

"And what's wrong with your home, I should like to know?" demanded Edith.

"I don't know. Everything seems to have changed. Why has it changed, Edith?"

Edith said gently:

"You're growing up, you see?"

"Is that what it is?"

"It might be."

Edith went towards the door with her tray of glasses. Then, unexpectedly, she put it down and came back. She patted Sarah's black head, as she had patted it years ago in the nursery.

"There, there, my pretty, there, there."

With a sudden change of mood Sarah sprang up and catching Edith round the waist, began to waltz wildly round the room with her.

"I'm going to be married, Edith. Isn't it fun? I'm going to marry Mr. Steene. He's rolling in money and he's madly attractive. Aren't I a lucky girl?"

Edith extricated herself, grumbling. "First one thing and then another. What's the matter with you, Miss Sarah?"

"I'm a little mad, I think. You shall come to the wedding, Edith, and I'll buy you a lovely new dress for it—crimson velvet, if you like."

"What do you think a wedding is—a Coronation?"

Sarah put the tray into Edith's hands and pushed her towards the door.

"Go on, you old darling, and don't grumble."

Edith shook her head doubtfully as she went.

Sarah walked slowly back into the room. Suddenly she flung herself down into the big chair and cried and cried.

The gramophone record drew to its close—the deep melancholy voice singing once more—

Sometimes I feel like a motherless child—a long way from Home . . .

BOOK 3

Chapter one

Edith moved slowly and stiffly round her kitchen. She had been feeling what she called her "rheumatics" more and more lately, and it did not improve her temper. She still obstinately refused to delegate any of her household tasks.

A lady referred to by Edith as *"that* Mrs. Hopper," with a sniff, was allowed to come once a week and perform certain activities under Edith's jealous eye, but any further help was negatived by her with a venom that boded ill for any cleaning woman who dared to attempt it.

"I've always managed, haven't I?" was Edith's slogan.

So she continued to manage with an air of martyrdom and an increasingly sour expression. She had also formed the habit of grumbling under her breath most of the day.

She was doing so now.

"Bringing the milk at lunch-time—the idea! Milk should be delivered before breakfast, that's the proper time for it. Impudent young fellows, coming along whistling in their white coats . . . Who do they think they are? Look like whippersnapper dentists to me . . ."

The sound of the latch-key in the front door arrested the flow.

Edith murmured to herself. "Now there'll be ructions!" and rinsed out a bowl under the tap with a vicious swishing motion.

Ann's voice called:

"Edith."

Edith removed her hands from the sink and dried them meticulously on the roller towel.

"Edith . . . Edith . . ."

"Coming, ma'am."

"Edith!"

Edith raised her eyebrows, pulled down the corners of her mouth and went out of the kitchen across the hall into the sitting-room where Ann Prentice was tossing through letters and bills. She turned as Edith entered.

"Did you ring up Dame Laura?"

"Yes, of course I did."

Ann said: "Did you tell her it was urgent—that I *must* see her? Did she say she'd come?"

"Said she'd be round right away."

"Well, why hasn't she come?" demanded Ann angrily.

"I only telephoned twenty minutes ago. Just after you went out."

"It feels like an hour. Why doesn't she come?"

Edith said, in a more soothing tone:

"Everything can't happen right away. It's no good your upsetting yourself."

"Did you tell her I was ill?"

"I told her you was in one of your states."

Ann said angrily: "What do you mean—one of my states? It's my nerves. They're all to pieces."

"That's right, they are."

Ann threw her faithful retainer an angry glance. She walked restlessly over to the window, then to the mantelpiece. Edith stood watching her, her big awkward jointed hands, seamed with work, moving up and down on her apron.

"I can't stay still a moment," Ann complained. "I didn't sleep a wink last night. I feel terrible—terrible . . ." She sat down in a chair and put both hands to her temples. "I don't know what's the matter with me."

"I do," said Edith. "Too much gadding about. 'Tisn't natural at your age."

"Edith!" cried Ann. "You're very impertinent. You're getting worse and worse lately. You've been with me a long time and I value your services, but if you're going to presume you'll have to go."

Edith raised her eyes to the ceiling and assumed her martyr's expression.

She said: "I'm not going. And that's flat."

"You'll go if I give you notice," said Ann.

"You'd be more foolish than I think you are if you did a thing like that. I'd get another place easy as winking. Running after me they'd be, at these domestic agencies. But how would *you* get along? Nothing but daily women as likely as not! Or else a foreigner. Everything cooked in oil and turning your stomach—to say nothing of the smell in the flat. And those foreigners aren't so good on the telephone—get every name wrong, they would. Or else you'd get a nice clean pleasant-spoken woman, too good to be true, and you'd come back one day to find she'd made off with your furs and your jewellery. Heard of a case in Playne Court opposite only the other day. No, you're one as has to have things done the proper way—the *old* way. I cook you nice little meals and I don't go smashing your pretty things when I wash up, as some of these young hussies do, and what's more I know your ways. You can't do without me, and I know it, and I'm not going. Trying you may be, but everyone's got his cross to bear. It says so in Holy Writ, and you're mine and I'm a Christian woman."

Ann clasped her eyes and rocked to and fro with a moan. "Oh, my head—my *head* . . ."

Edith's rigid sourness softened—a tenderness showed in her eyes.

"There, now. I'll make you a nice cup of tea."

Ann cried pettishly: "I don't want a nice cup of tea. I'd hate a nice cup of tea."

Edith sighed and raised her eyes to the ceiling once more. "Please yourself," she said and left the room.

Ann reached for the cigarette box, took one out, lit it, puffed at it for a moment or two and then stubbed it out in the ash-tray. She got up and started pacing about again.

After a minute or so she went to the telephone and dialled a number.

"Hullo—hullo—can I speak to Lady Ladscombe—oh, is that you, Marcia darling?" Her voice assumed an artificially gay note. "How are you? . . . Oh, nothing really. I just thought I'd ring you up. . . . I don't know, darling—just felt frightfully blue—you know how one does. Are you doing anything tomorrow for lunch? . . . Oh, I see . . . Thursday night? Yes, I'm quite free. That would be lovely. I'll get hold of Lee or somebody and get up a party. That will be wonderful . . . I'll give you a ring in the morning."

She rang off. Her momentary animation subsided. Once again she began pacing about. Then, as she heard the door-bell, she stood still, poised in expectancy.

She heard Edith say:

"She's waiting for you in the sitting-room," and then Laura Whitstable came in. Tall, grim, forbidding, but with the comfortable steadfastness of a rock in the middle of a heaving sea.

Ann ran towards her, crying out incoherently and with rising hysteria.

"Oh, Laura—*Laura*—I'm so glad you've come . . ."

Dame Laura's eyebrows went up, her eyes were steady and watchful. She laid her hands on Ann's shoulders and steered her gently to the couch where she sat down beside her, saying as she did so:

"Well, well, what's all this?"

Ann still sounded hysterical.

"Oh, I'm *so* glad to see you. I think I'm going mad."

"Nonsense," said Dame Laura robustly. "What's the trouble?"

"Nothing. Nothing at all. It's just my nerves. That's what frightens me. I can't sit still. I don't know what's the matter with me."

"H'm," Laura gave her a searching professional look. "You don't look too well."

Secretly she was dismayed by Ann's appearance. Under the heavy make-up Ann's face was haggard. She looked years older than when Laura had seen her last, some months ago.

Ann said fretfully: "I'm perfectly *well*. It's just—I don't know what it is. I can't sleep—not unless I take things. And I'm so irritable and bad tempered."

"Seen a doctor?"

"Not lately. They just give you bromide and tell you not to overdo things."

"Very good advice."

"Yes, but it's all so absurd. I've *never* been a nervy woman, Laura, you know I haven't. I've never known what nerves were."

Laura Whitstable was silent for a moment, remembering the Ann Prentice of just over three years ago. Her gentle placidity, her repose, her enjoyment of life, her sweetness and evenness of temper. She felt deeply grieved for this friend of hers.

She said:

"It's all very well to say you've never been a nervy woman. After all, a man who has a broken leg has very likely never had a broken leg before!"

"But why should *I* have nerves?"

Laura Whitstable was careful in her answer.

She said evenly: "Your doctor was right. You probably do too much."

Ann said sharply:

"I can't sit at home moping all day."

"There's such a thing as sitting home without moping," said Dame Laura.

"No," Ann's hands fluttered nervously. "I—I can't sit about and do nothing."

"Why not?" The question came sharp as a probe.

"I don't know." Ann's fluttering increased. "I can't be alone. I can't . . ." She threw a despairing glance at Laura. "I suppose you'd think I was quite mad if I said I was *afraid* of being alone?"

"Most sensible thing you've said yet," returned Dame Laura promptly.

"Sensible?" Ann was startled.

"Yes, because it's the truth."

"The truth?" Ann's eyelids fell. "I don't know what you mean by the truth."

"I mean that we shan't get anywhere without the truth."

"Oh, but you won't be able to understand. You've never been afraid of being alone, have you?"

"No."

"Then you just can't understand."

"Oh yes, I can." Laura went on gently: "Why did you send for me, my dear?"

"I had to talk to someone . . . I had to . . . and I thought perhaps you could *do* something?"

She looked hopefully at her friend.

Laura nodded her head and sighed.

"I see. You want a conjuring trick."

"Couldn't you do one for me, Laura? Psycho-analysis, or hypnotism, or *something.*"

"Mumbo jumbo in modern terms, in fact?" Laura shook her head decisively. "I can't take the rabbits out of the hat for you, Ann. You must do that for yourself. And you've got to find out, first, exactly what's in the hat."

"What do you mean?"

Laura Whitstable waited a minute before saying: "You're not happy, Ann."

It was a statement rather than a question.

Ann replied quickly, too quickly perhaps.

"Oh yes, I am—at least I am in a way. I enjoy myself a good deal."

"You're not happy," said Dame Laura ruthlessly.

Ann made a gesture with her shoulders and her hands.

"Is anybody happy?" she threw out.

"Quite a lot of people are, thank God," said Dame Laura cheerfully. *"Why* aren't you happy, Ann?"

"I don't know."

"Nothing's going to help you but the truth, Ann. You know the answer quite well really."

Ann was silent a moment, then as though taking her courage in her hands, she burst out:

"I suppose—if I'm to be honest—because I'm growing old. I'm middle-aged, I'm losing my looks, I've nothing to look forward to in the future."

"Oh, my dear! Nothing to look forward to? You've excellent health, adequate brains—there is so much in life that one hasn't really time to attend to until one is past middle-age. I told you so once. Books, flowers, music, pictures, people, sunshine—all the interwoven inextricable pattern that we call Life."

Ann was silent a moment, then she said defiantly:

"Oh I daresay it's all a question of sex. Nothing else really matters when one isn't attractive to men any longer."

"That is possibly true of some women. It isn't true of you, Ann. You've seen the 'Immortal Hour'—or read it perhaps? Do you remember those lines: *'There is an Hour wherein a man might be happy all his life could he but find it'?* You came near to finding it once, didn't you?"

Ann's face changed—softened. She looked suddenly a much younger woman.

She murmured: "Yes. There was that hour. I could have known it with Richard. I could have grown old happily with Richard."

Laura said with deep sympathy:

"I know."

Ann went on. "And now—I can't even regret losing him! I saw him again, you know—oh, just about a year ago—and he meant nothing to me at all—*nothing.* That's what's so tragic, so absurd. It had all gone. We meant nothing to each other any more. He was just an ordinary middle-aged man— a little pompous, rather dull, inclined to be fatuous about his new, pretty, empty-headed meretricious little wife. Quite nice, you know, yet definitely boring. And yet—and yet—if we had married—I think we'd have been happy together. I *know* we should have been happy."

"Yes," said Laura thoughtfully, "I think you would."

"I was so near happiness—so near it—" Ann's voice trembled with self-pity—"and then—I had to let it all go."

"Had you?"

Ann paid no attention to the question.

"I gave it all up—for Sarah!"

"Exactly," said Dame Laura. *"And you've never forgiven her for it, have you?"*

Ann came out of her dream—startled.

"What do you mean?"

Laura Whitstable gave a venomous snort.

"Sacrifices! Blood sacrifices! Just realise for a moment, Ann, what a sacrifice *means*. It isn't just the one heroic moment when you feel warmed and generous and willing to immolate yourself. The kind of sacrifice where you offer your breast to the knife is easy—for it ends there, in the moment when you are *greater than yourself*. But most sacrifices you have to live with *afterwards*—all day and every day —and that's *not* so easy. One has to be very big for that. You, Ann, weren't quite big enough . . ."

Ann flushed angrily.

"I gave up my whole life, my one chance of happiness, for Sarah's sake, and all you say is that it wasn't enough!"

"That isn't what I said."

"Everything's *my* fault, I suppose!" Ann was still angry.

Dame Laura said earnestly: "Half the troubles in life come from pretending to oneself that one is a better and finer human being than one is."

But Ann was not listening. Her unassimilated resentment came pouring out.

"Sarah's just like all these modern girls, wrapped up in herself. Never thinks of anybody else! Do you know that just over a year ago, when he rang up, she didn't even remember who Richard was? His name meant nothing to her—nothing at all."

Laura Whitstable nodded her head gravely with the air of one who sees her diagnosis proved correct.

"I see," she said. "I see . . ."

Ann went on: "What could I do? They never stopped fighting. It was nerve-racking! If I'd gone on with it there wouldn't have been a moment's peace."

Laura Whitstable spoke crisply and unexpectedly:

"If I were you, Ann, I should make up your mind whether you gave up Richard Cauldfield for Sarah's sake, or for the sake of your own peace."

Ann looked at her resentfully.

"I loved Richard," she said, "but I loved Sarah more. . . ."

"No, Ann, it isn't nearly as simple as that. I think that there was actually a moment when you loved Richard better than you loved Sarah. I think your inner unhappiness and resentment springs from that moment. If you'd given up Richard because you loved Sarah more, you wouldn't be in the state you are today. But if you gave up Richard out of weakness, because Sarah bullied you—because you wanted to escape from the bickering and the quarrels, if it was a defeat and *not* a renunciation—well, that's a thing one never likes admitting to oneself. But you did care for Richard very deeply."

Ann said bitterly:

"And now he means nothing to me!"

"What about Sarah?"

"Sarah?"

"Yes. What does Sarah mean to you?"

Ann shrugged her shoulders.

"Since her marriage I've hardly seen her. She's very busy and gay, I believe. But as I say, I hardly see anything of her."

"*I* saw her last night . . ." Laura paused, then went on: "In a restaurant with a party of people." She paused again and then said bluntly: "She was drunk."

"Drunk?" Ann sounded momentarily startled. Then she laughed. "Laura dear, you mustn't be old-fashioned. All young people drink a good deal nowadays, and it seems a party's hardly a success unless everybody's half-seas over, or 'high' or whatever you like to call it."

Laura was unruffled.

"That may be so—and I admit I'm old-fashioned enough not to like seeing a young woman I know drunk in a public place. But there's more than that, Ann. I spoke to Sarah. The pupils of her eyes were dilated."

"What does that mean?"

"One of the things it *could* mean is cocaine."

"Drugs?"

"Yes. I told you once that I suspected Lawrence Steene was mixed up with the drug racket. Oh, not for money—purely for sensation."

"He always seems quite normal."

"Oh, drugs won't hurt him. I know his type. They enjoy experimenting with sensation. His sort don't become addicts. A woman's different. If a woman's unhappy, these things get a hold on her—a hold that she can't break."

"Unhappy?" Ann sounded incredulous. "Sarah?"

Watching her closely, Laura Whitstable said dryly:

"You should know. You're her mother."

"Oh, *that!* Sarah doesn't confide in me."

"Why not?"

Ann got up, went over to the window, then came back slowly towards the fireplace. Dame Laura sat quite still and watched her. As Ann lit a cigarette, Laura asked quietly:

"What does it mean to you exactly, Ann, that Sarah should be unhappy?"

"How can you ask? It upsets me—terribly."

"Does it?" Laura rose. "Well, I must be going. I've got a committee meeting in ten minutes' time. I can just make it."

She went towards the door. Ann followed her.

"What do you mean by saying 'Does it?' like that, Laura?"

"I had some gloves somewhere— Now where did I put them?"

The bell of the front door sounded. Edith padded out of the kitchen to answer it.

Ann persisted: "You meant *something?*"

"Ah, here they are."

"Really, Laura, I think you're being horrible to me—quite horrible!"

Edith came in announcing with something that might almost have been a smile:

"Now here's a stranger. It's Mr. Lloyd, ma'am."

Ann stared at Gerry Lloyd for a moment as though she could hardly take him in.

It was over three years since she had seen him and Gerry looked a good deal more than three years older. He had a battered look about him, and his face showed the tired lines of the unsuccessful. He was wearing a rather rough country tweed suit, obviously a reach-me-down, and his shoes were shabby. It was clear that he had not prospered. The smile with which he greeted her was a grave one and his whole manner was serious, not to say perturbed.

"Gerry, this *is* a surprise!"

"It's good that you remember me, anyway. Three and a half years is a long time."

"I remember you, too, young man, but I don't suppose you remember me," said Dame Laura.

"Oh, but of course I do, Dame Laura. No one could forget *you*."

"Nicely put—or isn't it? Well, I must be on my way. Good-bye, Ann; good-bye, Mr. Lloyd."

She went out and Gerry followed Ann over to the fireplace. He sat down and took the cigarette she offered him.

Ann spoke gaily and cheerfully.

"Well, Gerry, tell me all about yourself and what you have been doing. Are you in England for long?"

"I'm not sure."

His level gaze, fixed on her, made Ann feel slightly uncomfortable. She wondered what was in his mind. It was a look very unlike the Gerry she remembered.

"Have a drink. What will you have—gin and orange—or pink gin—?"

"No, thanks. I don't want one. I came—just to talk to you."

"How nice of you. Have you seen Sarah? She's married, you know. To a man called Lawrence Steene."

"I know that. She wrote and told me. And I've seen her. I saw her last night. That's really why I've come here to see you." He paused for a moment and then said: "Mrs. Prentice, why did you let her marry that man?"

Ann was taken back.

"Gerry, my dear—*really!*"

His earnestness was unabated by her protest. He spoke seriously and quite simply.

"She isn't happy. You know that, don't you? She isn't happy."

"Did she tell you so?"

"No, of course not. Sarah wouldn't do a thing like that.

It wasn't necessary to tell me. I saw it at once. She was with a crowd of people—I only had a few words with her. But it sticks out a mile. Mrs. Prentice, why did you let such a thing happen?"

Ann felt her anger rising.

"My dear Gerry, aren't you being rather absurd?"

"No, I don't think so." He considered a moment. His complete simplicity and sincerity were disarming. "You see, Sarah matters to me. She always has. More than anything else in the world. So naturally I care whether she's happy or not. You know, you really shouldn't have let her marry Steene."

Ann broke out angrily:

"Really, Gerry, you talk like—like a Victorian. There was no question of my 'letting' or 'not letting' Sarah marry Larry Steene. Girls marry whoever they choose to marry and there's nothing their parents can do about it. Sarah chose to marry Lawrence Steene. That's all there is to it."

Gerry said with calm certainty:

"You could have stopped it."

"My dear boy, if you try to stop people doing what they want to do, it just makes them more obstinate and pigheaded."

He raised his eyes to her face.

"Did you try to stop it?"

Somehow, under the frank inquiry of those eyes, Ann floundered and stammered.

"I—I—of course he was much older than she was—and his reputation wasn't good. I did point that out to her—but—"

"He's a swine of the worst description."

"You can't really know anything about him, Gerry. You've been out of England for years."

"It's pretty common knowledge. Everybody knows. I daresay you wouldn't know all the unpleasant details—but surely, Mrs. Prentice, you must have *felt* the kind of brute he is?"

"He was always very charming and pleasant to me," said Ann defensively, "And a man with a past doesn't always turn out such a bad husband. You can't believe all the spiteful things people say. Sarah was attracted by him—in fact she was determined to marry him. He's exceedingly well off—"

Gerry interrupted her.

"Yes, he's well off. But you're not the kind of woman, Mrs. Prentice, who just wants her daughter to marry for money. You were never what I'd call—well—worldly. You would just have wanted Sarah to be happy—or so I should have thought."

He looked at her with a kind of puzzled curiosity.

"Of course I wanted my only child to be happy. That goes without saying. But the point is, Gerry, that one can't *interfere*." She laboured the point. "You may think that what anyone is doing is all wrong, but you can't interfere."

She gazed at him defiantly.

He looked at her, still with that thoughtful, considering air.

"Did Sarah really want to marry him so much?"

"She was very much in love with him," Ann said defiantly. When Gerry did not speak, she went on:

"I don't expect it's apparent to you, but Lawrence is exceedingly attractive to women."

"Oh yes, I quite realise that."

Ann rallied herself.

"You know, Gerry," she said, "you're really being quite unreasonable. Just because there was once a boy-and-girl thing between you and Sarah, you come here and accuse me —as though Sarah's marrying someone else was my fault—"

He interrupted her.

"I think it *was* your fault."

They stared at each other. Colour rose in Gerry's face, Ann grew pale. The tension between them was strained to breaking point.

Ann got up. "This is too much," she said coldly.

Gerry rose too. He was quiet and polite, but she was aware of something implacable and remorseless behind the quietness of his manner.

"I'm sorry," he said, "if I've been rude—"

"It's unpardonable!"

"Perhaps it is, in a way. But you see I mind about Sarah.

She's the only thing I do mind about. I can't help feeling that you've let her in for an unhappy marriage."

"Really!"

"I'm going to take her out of it."

"What?"

"I'm going to persuade her to leave that swine."

"What absolute nonsense. Just because there was once this girl-and-boy love affair between you two——"

"I understand Sarah—and she understands me."

Ann gave a sudden hard laugh.

"My dear Gerry, you'll find that Sarah has changed a good deal since you used to know her."

Gerry went very pale.

"I know she's changed," he said in a low voice. "I saw that. . . ."

He hesitated a moment, then said quietly:

"I'm sorry if you feel I've been impertinent, Mrs. Prentice. But you see, with me, Sarah will always come first."

He went out of the room.

Ann moved over to the drinks and poured herself out a glass of gin. As she drank it she murmured to herself:

"How dare he—how dare he . . . And Laura—*she's* against me too. They're all against me. It isn't fair . . . What have I done? Nothing at all. . . ."

Chapter two

1

The butler who opened the door of 18 Pauncefoot Square looked superciliously at Gerry's ready-made rough suit.

Then, as his eye was caught by the visitor's eye, his manner underwent reconsideration.

He would find out, he said, if Mrs. Steene was at home.

Shortly afterwards Gerry was ushered into a large dim room full of exotic flowers and pale brocades, and here, after a lapse of some minutes, Sarah Steene came into the room, smiling a greeting.

"Well, Gerry! How nice of you to look me up. We were snatched away from each other the other night. Drink?"

She fetched him a drink and poured herself one, and then came to sit on a low *pouf* by the fire. The soft lighting of the room hardly showed her face. She had on some expensive perfume that he did not remember her using.

"Well, Gerry?" she said again, lightly.

He smiled back.

"Well, Sarah?"

Then with a finger touching her shoulder, he said: "Practically wearing the Zoo, aren't you?"

She had on an expensive wisp of chiffon trimmed with masses of soft pale fur.

"Nice!" Sarah assured him.

"Yes. You look wonderfully expensive!"

"Oh, I am. Now, Gerry, tell me the news. You left South Africa and went to Kenya. Since then, I've heard nothing at all."

"Oh, well. I've been rather down on my luck—"

"Naturally—"

The retort came swiftly.

Gerry demanded:

"What do you mean—naturally?"

"Well, luck always was your trouble, wasn't it?"

Just for a moment it was the old Sarah, teasing, hard-hitting. The beautiful woman with the hard face, the exotic stranger, was gone. It was Sarah, his Sarah, attacking him shrewdly.

And responding in his old manner, he grumbled:

"One thing after another let me down. First it was the crops that failed—no fault of mine. Then the cattle got disease—"

"I know. The old, old sad story."

"And then, of course, I hadn't enough capital. If only I'd had capital—"

"I know—I know."

"Well, dash it all, Sarah, it's *not* all my fault."

"It never is. What have you come back to England for?"

"As a matter of fact, my aunt died—"

"Aunt Lena?" asked Sarah, who was well acquainted with all Gerry's relatives.

"Yes. Uncle Luke died two years ago. The old screw never left me a penny—"

"Wise Uncle Luke."

"But Aunt Lena—"

"Aunt Lena has left you something?"

"Yes. Ten thousand pounds."

"H'm." Sarah considered. "That's not so bad—even in these days."

"I'm going in with a fellow who's got a ranch in Canada."

"What sort of a fellow? That's always the point. What about the garage you were starting with another fellow after you left South Africa?"

"Oh, that petered out. We did quite well to start with, but then we enlarged up a bit, and a slump came—"

"You needn't tell me. How familiar the pattern is! *Your* pattern."

"Yes," said Gerry. He added simply: "You're quite right, I suppose, I'm not really much good. I still think I've had rotten luck—but I suppose I've played the fool a bit as well. However, this time is going to be different."

Sarah said bitingly:

"I wonder."

"Come, Sarah. Don't you think I've learned a lesson?"

"I shouldn't think so," said Sarah. "People never do. They go on repeating themselves. What you need, Gerry, is a manager—like film stars and actresses. Someone to be practical and save you from being optimistic at the wrong moment."

"You've got something there. But really, Sarah, it will be all right this time. I'm going to be damn careful."

There was a pause and then Gerry said:

"I went and saw your mother yesterday."

"Did you? How nice of you. How was she? Rushing about madly as usual?"

Gerry said slowly: "Your mother's changed a lot."

"Do you think so?"

"Yes, I do."

"In what way do you think she's changed?"

"I don't quite know how to put it." He hesitated. "She's frightfully nervy, for one thing."

Sarah said lightly: "Who isn't in these days?"

"She used not to be. She was always calm and—and—well —*sweet.* . . ."

"Sounds like a line of a hymn!"

"You know what I mean quite well—and she *has* changed. Her hair—and her clothes—everything."

"She's gone a bit gay, that's all. Why shouldn't she, poor darling? Getting old must be absolutely the end! Anyway, people do change." Sarah paused for a minute before adding with a touch of defiance in her voice: "I expect *I*'ve changed, too. . . ."

"Not really."

Sarah flushed. Gerry said deliberately:

"In spite of the zoo," he touched the pale expensive fur again, "and the Woolworth assortment," he touched a diamond spray on her shoulder, "and the luxury setting—you're pretty much the same Sarah—" He paused and added: *"My* Sarah."

Sarah moved uncomfortably. She said in a gay voice:

"And you're still the same old Gerry. When do you go off to Canada?"

"Quite soon now. As soon as all the lawyer's business is cleared up."

He rose. "Well, I must be off. Come out with me some day soon, will you, Sarah?"

"No, you come and dine here with us. Or we'll have a party. You must meet Larry."

"I met him the other night, didn't I?"

"Only for a moment."

"I'm afraid I haven't time for parties. Come out for a walk with me one morning, Sarah."

"Darling, I'm really not up to much in the morning. A hideous time of day."

"A very good time for cold clear thinking."

"Who wants to do any cold clear thinking?"

"I think *we* do. Come on, Sarah. Twice round Regent's Park. And tomorrow morning. I'll meet you at Hanover Gate."

"You do have the most hideous ideas, Gerry! And what an awful suit."

"Very hard wearing."

"Yes, but the cut of it!"

"Clothes snob! Tomorrow, twelve o'clock, Hanover Gate. And don't get so tight tonight that you'll have a hangover tomorrow."

"I suppose you mean I was tight last night?"

"Well, you were, weren't you?"

"It was such a dreary party. Drink does help a girl through."

Gerry reiterated:

"Tomorrow. Hanover Gate. Twelve o'clock."

2

"Well, I've come," said Sarah, defiantly.

Gerry looked her up and down. She was astonishingly beautiful—far more beautiful than she had been as a girl. He noted the expensive simplicity of the clothes she was wearing, the big cabuchon emerald on her finger. He thought: "I'm mad." But he did not waver.

"Come on," he said. "We walk."

He walked her briskly, too. They skirted the lake and passed through the rose garden and paused at last to sit in two chairs in an unfrequented part of the park. It was too cold for there to be many people sitting about.

Gerry took a deep breath.

"Now," he said, "we get down to things. Sarah, will you come with me to Canada?"

Sarah stared at him in amazement.

"What on earth do you mean?"

"Just what I say."

"Do you mean—a kind of trip?" Sarah asked doubtfully.

Gerry grinned.

"I mean for good. Leave your husband and come to me."

Sarah laughed.

"Gerry, are you quite mad? Why, we haven't seen each other for nearly four years and—"

"Does that matter?"

"No." Sarah was taken off her balance. "No, I suppose it doesn't. . . ."

"Four years, five years, ten, twenty? I don't believe it would make any difference. You and I belong together. I've always known that. I still feel it. Don't you feel it, too?"

"Yes, in a way," Sarah admitted. "But all the same what you're suggesting is quite impossible."

"I don't see anything impossible about it. If you were married to some decent fellow and were happy with him, I shouldn't dream of butting in." He said in a low voice: "But you're not happy, are you, Sarah?"

"I'm as happy as most people, I suppose," said Sarah valiantly.

"I think you're utterly miserable."

"If I am—it's my own doing. After all, if one makes a mistake, one's got to abide by it."

"Lawrence Steene isn't particularly noticeable for abiding by his mistakes, is he?"

"That's a mean thing to say!"

"No, it isn't. It's true."

"And anyway, Gerry, what you suggest is quite, *quite* mad. Crazy!"

"Because I haven't hung round you and led up to it gradually? There's no need for that. As I say, you and I belong—and you know it, Sarah."

Sarah sighed.

"I was terribly fond of you once, I'll admit."

"It goes deeper than that, my girl."

She turned to look at him. Her pretences fell away.

"Does it? Are you sure?"

"I'm sure."

They were both silent. Then Gerry said gently:

"Will you come with me, Sarah?"

Sarah sighed. She sat up, pulling her furs more closely about her. There was a cold little breeze stirring the trees.

"Sorry, Gerry. The answer is No."

"Why?"

"I just can't do it—that's all."

"People are leaving their husbands every day."

"Not me."

"Are you telling me that you love Lawrence Steene?"
Sarah shook her head.

"No, I don't love him. I never did love him. He fascinated
me, though. He's—well, he's clever with women." She gave
a faint shiver of distaste. "One doesn't often feel that anybody is really—well—bad. But if I felt that about anybody
I'd feel it about Lawrence. Because the things he does aren't
hot-blooded things—they're not things he does because he
can't help doing them. He just likes experimenting with
people and things."

"Then need you have any scruples about leaving him?"

Sarah was silent for a moment, then she said in a low
voice:

"It's not scruples. Oh," she caught herself up impatiently,
"how disgusting it is that one always trots out one's noble
reasons first! All right, Gerry, you'd better know what I'm
really like. Living with Lawrence I've got used to—to certain
things. I don't want to give them up. Clothes, furs, money,
expensive restaurants, parties, a maid, cars, a yacht. . . .
Everything made easy and luxurious. I'm steeped in luxury.
And you want me to come and rough it on a ranch miles
from anywhere. I can't—and I won't. I've gone soft! I'm
rotted with money and luxury."

Gerry said unemotionally:

"Then it's about time you were hauled out of it all."

"Oh, Gerry!" Sarah was halfway between tears and
laughter. "You're so matter-of-fact."

"I've got my feet on the ground all right."

"Yes, but you don't understand half of it."

"No?"

"It's not only—just—money. It's other things. Oh, don't
you understand? I've become a rather horrible person. The
parties we have—and the places we go—"

She paused, crimsoning.

"All right," said Gerry calmly. "You're depraved. Anything else?"

"Yes. There are things—things I've got used to—things I just couldn't do without."

"Things?" He took her sharply by the chin, turned her head towards him. "I'd heard rumors. You mean—dope?"

Sarah nodded. "It gives you such wonderful sensations."

"Listen." Gerry's voice was hard and incisive. "You'll come with me, and you'll cut out all that stuff."

"Suppose I can't?"

"I'll see to that," said Gerry grimly.

Sarah's shoulders relaxed. She sighed, leaning towards him. But Gerry drew back.

"No," he said. "I'm not going to kiss you."

"I see. I've got to decide—in cold blood?"

"Yes."

"Funny Gerry!"

They sat silent for a few moments. Then Gerry said, speaking with rather an effort:

"I know all right that I'm not much good. I've made a mess of things all round. I do realise that you can't have much—faith in me. But I do believe, honestly I do, that if I had you with me I could put up a better show. You're so shrewd, Sarah. And you know how to ginger a fellow up when he's getting slack."

"I sound an adorable creature!" said Sarah.

Gerry insisted stubbornly:

"I know I can make good. It will be a hell of a life for you. Hard work and pigging it—yes, pretty fair hell. I don't know how I've got the cheek to persuade you to come. But it will be *real*, Sarah. It will be—well—*living*. . . ."

"Living . . . real . . ." Sarah repeated the words over to herself.

She got up and began to walk away. Gerry walked beside her.

"You'll come, Sarah?"

"I don't know."

"Sarah—darling . . ."

"No, Gerry—don't say any more. You've said it all—everything that needs to be said. It's up to me now. I've got to think. I'll let you know . . ."

"When?"

"Soon. . . ."

Chapter three

"Well, here's a nice surprise!"

Edith, opening the door of the flat to Sarah, creased the sour lines of her face into a dour smile.

"Hullo, Edith, my pet. Mother in?"

"I'm expecting her any minute now. I'm glad you've come. Cheer her up a bit."

"Does she need cheering up? She always sounds frightfully gay."

"There's something very wrong with your mother. Worried about her, I am." Edith followed Sarah into the sitting-room. "Can't keep still for two minutes together and snaps your head off if you so much as make a remark. Organic, I shouldn't wonder."

"Oh, don't croak, Edith. According to you everyone is always at death's door."

"I shan't say it of you, Miss Sarah. Blooming, you're looking. Tch!—dropping your lovely furs about on the floor. That's you all over. Lovely they are, must have cost a mint of money."

"They cost the earth all right."

"Nicer than any the mistress ever had. You certainly have got a lot of lovely things, Miss Sarah."

"So I should have. If you sell your soul, you've got to get a good price for it."

"That's not a nice way to talk," said Edith disapprovingly. "The worst of you is, Miss Sarah, that you're up and down. How well I remember as though it was yesterday, here in this very room, when you told me you was hoping to marry Mr.

Steene, and how you danced me round the room like a mad thing. 'I'm going to be married—I'm going to be married,' you said."

Sarah said sharply: "Don't—don't, Edith. I can't stand it."

Edith's face became immediately alert and knowledgeable.

"There, there, dearie," she said soothingly. "The first two years is always the worst, they say. If you can weather them, you'll be all right."

"Hardly a very optimistic view of marriage."

Edith said disapprovingly: "Marriage is a poor business at best, but I suppose the world couldn't get on without it. You'll excuse the liberty, no little strangers on the way?"

"No, there are *not*, Edith."

"Sorry, I'm sure. But you seemed a bit on edge like, and I wondered if that mightn't be the reason. Very odd the way young married ladies behave sometimes. My elder sister, when she was expecting, she was in the grocer's shop one day and it came to her sudden like as she must have a great big juicy pear as was there in a case. Seized it, she did, and bit into it then and there. 'Here, what are you doing?' the young assistant said. But the grocer, he was a family man, and he understood how it was. 'That'll do, sonny,' he says, 'I'll attend to this lady'—and he didn't charge her for it, either. Very understanding he was, having thirteen of his own."

"How unlucky to have thirteen children," said Sarah. "What a wonderful family you have got, Edith. I've heard about them ever since I was a little girl."

"Ah, yes. Many's the story I've told you. Such a serious little thing as you were, and minding so much about everything. And that reminds me, that young gentleman of yours was round here the other day. Mr. Lloyd. Have you seen him?"

"Yes, I've seen him."

"Looks much older—but beautifully sunburnt. That comes from being so much in foreign parts. Done well for himself, has he?"

"Not particularly."

"Ah, that's a pity. Not quite enough drive to him—that's what's the matter with him."

"I suppose it is. Do you think Mother will be coming soon?"

"Oh, yes, Miss Sarah. She's going out to dinner. So she'll be home to change first. If you ask me, Miss Sarah, it's a great pity she doesn't have more quiet nights at home. She does far too much."

"I suppose she enjoys it."

"All this rushing around." Edith sniffed. "It doesn't suit her. She was always a quiet lady."

Sarah turned her head sharply, as though Edith's words had struck some chord of remembrance. She repeated musingly:

"A quiet lady. Yes, Mother was quiet. Gerry said so too. Funny how she's altered completely in the last three years. Do *you* think she's changed a lot, Edith?"

"Sometimes I'd say she wasn't the same lady."

"She used to be quite different . . . She used to be—" Sarah broke off, thinking. Then she went on: "Do you think mothers always go on being fond of their children, Edith?"

"Of course they do, Miss Sarah. It wouldn't be natural if they didn't."

"But is it really natural to go on caring about your young once they're grown up and out in the world? Animals don't."

Edith was scandalised. She said sharply:

"Animals indeed! We're Christian men and women. Don't you talk nonsense, Miss Sarah. Remember the saying: *A son's a son till he gets him a wife. But a daughter's a daughter all your life.*"

Sarah laughed.

"I know heaps of mothers who hate their daughters like poison, and daughters who've got no use for their mothers, either."

"Well, all I can say is, Miss Sarah, that I don't think that's at all nice."

"But much, much healthier, Edith—or so our psychologists say."

"Nasty minds they've got, then."

Sarah said thoughtfully:

"I've always been frightfully fond of Mother—as a person—not as a mother."

"And your mother's devoted to you, Miss Sarah."

Sarah did not answer for some seconds. Then she said thoughtfully: "I wonder . . ."

Edith sniffed.

"If you knew the state she was in when you had the pneumonia when you were fourteen—"

"Oh, yes, *then*. But now . . ."

They both heard the sound of the latch-key. Edith said: "Here she is now."

Ann came in breathlessly, pulling off a gay little hat of multi-coloured feathers.

"Sarah? What a nice surprise. Oh dear, this hat has been hurting my head. What's the time? I'm terribly late. I'm meeting the Ladesburys at Chaliano's at eight. Come into my room while I change."

Sarah followed her obediently along the passage, and into her bedroom.

"How's Lawrence?" Ann asked.

"Very well."

"Good. Its ages since I've seen him—or you either for that matter. We must have a party sometime. That new revue at the Coronation sounds quite good—"

"Mother. I want to talk to you."

"Yes, darling?"

"Can't you stop doing things to your face and just listen to me?"

Ann looked surprised.

"Dear me, Sarah. You seem very much on edge."

"I want to talk to you. It's serious. It's—Gerry."

"Oh." Ann's hands fell to her sides. She looked thoughtful. "Gerry?"

Sarah said baldly:

"He wants me to leave Lawrence and go to Canada with him."

Ann breathed in once or twice. Then she said lightly:

"What absolute nonsense! Poor old Gerry. He really is too stupid for words."

Sarah said sharply:

"Gerry's all right."

Ann said: "I know you've always stuck up for him, darling. But seriously, don't you find you've rather outgrown him now that you see him again?"

"You're not helping me much, Mother," said Sarah. Her voice shook a little. "I want to be—serious about it."

Ann said sharply:

"You're not taking this ridiculous nonsense seriously?"

"Yes, I am."

Ann said angrily: "Then you're being stupid, Sarah."

Sarah said obstinately: "I've always cared for Gerry and he for me."

Ann laughed.

"Oh, my dear child!"

"I ought never to have married Lawrence. It was the greatest mistake I ever made."

"You'll settle down," said Ann comfortably.

Sarah got up and prowled up and down restlessly.

"I shan't. I shan't. My life's hell—pure hell."

"Don't exaggerate, Sarah." Ann's voice was acid.

"He's a beast—an inhuman beast."

"He's devoted to you Sarah," said Ann reproachfully.

"Why did I do it? Why? I never really wanted to marry him." She whirled round suddenly on Ann. "I shouldn't have married him if it hadn't been for *you*."

"Me?" Ann flushed angrily. "I had nothing to do with it!"

"You did—you did!"

"I told you at the time you must make up your own mind."

"You persuaded me it would be all right."

"What wicked nonsense! Why, I told you he had a bad reputation, that you were taking a risk—"

"I know. But it was the *way* you said it. As though it didn't matter. Oh, the whole thing! I don't care what words you used. The words were all right. *But you wanted me to marry him*. You *did*, Mother. I *know* you did! Why? Because you wanted to get rid of me?"

Ann faced her daughter angrily.

"Really, Sarah, this is the most extraordinary attack."

Sarah came up close to her mother. Her eyes, enormous and dark in her white face, stared into Ann's face as though she were looking there for the truth.

"I know what I'm saying is true. *You wanted me to marry Lawrence*. And now it's turned out all wrong, now that I'm hellishly unhappy, you don't care. Sometimes—I've even thought you were *pleased* . . ."

"Sarah!"

"Yes, *pleased*." Her eyes were still searching. Ann was restless under that stare. "You *are* pleased. . . . You want me to be unhappy . . ."

Ann turned brusquely away. She was trembling. She walked away towards the door. Sarah followed her.

"Why? Why, Mother?"

Ann said, forcing the words through stiff lips:

"You don't know what you are saying."

Sarah persisted:

"I want to know why you wanted me to be unhappy."

"I never wanted you to be unhappy! Don't be absurd!"

"Mother . . ." Timidly, like a child, Sarah touched her mother's arm. "Mother . . . I'm your daughter . . . You ought to be fond of me."

"Of course I'm fond of you! What next?"

"No," said Sarah. "I don't think that you are. I don't think that you've been fond of me for a long time. . . . You've gone right away from me . . . somewhere where I can't get at you. . . ."

Ann made an effort to pull herself together. She said in a matter-of-fact voice:

"However much you care for your children, there comes a time when they have to learn to stand on their own feet. Mothers mustn't be possessive."

"No, of course not. But I think that when one is in trouble, one ought to be able to come to one's mother."

"But what do you want me to *do*, Sarah?"

"I want you to tell me whether I shall go away with Gerry or stay with Lawrence."

"Stay with your husband, of course."

"You sound very positive."

"My dear child, what other answer can you expect from a woman of my generation? I was brought up to observe certain standards of behaviour."

"Morally right to stay with a husband, morally wrong to go away with a lover! Is that it?"

"Exactly. Of course, I daresay your modern friends would quite take a different view. But you asked me for mine."

Sarah sighed and shook her head.

"It isn't nearly as simple as you make it sound. It's all mixed up. Actually, it's the nastiest Me that would like to stay with Lawrence—the Me that's afraid to risk poverty and difficulties—the Me that likes soft living—the Me that has depraved tastes and is a slave to sensation. . . . The other Me, the Me that wants to go with Gerry isn't just an amorous little slut—it's a Me that believes in Gerry and wants to help him. You see, Mother, I've got just that something that Gerry hasn't got. There's a moment when he sits down and pities himself and it's just then that he needs me to give him a terrific kick in the pants! Gerry could be a really fine sort of person—he's got it in him. He just wants someone to laugh at him, and goad him and—oh, he—he just wants *me*. . . ."

Sarah stopped and looked imploringly at Ann. Ann's face was set like flint.

"It's no good my pretending to be impressed, Sarah. You married Lawrence of your own free will, no matter what you pretend, and you ought to stick to him."

"Perhaps . . ."

Ann pressed her advantage.

"And you know, darling," her tone was affectionate, "I don't feel that you're really cut out for a life of roughing it. It sounds all right just talking about it, but I'm sure you'd hate it when it came to the point, especially—" this, she felt, was a good touch—"especially if you felt you were hampering Gerry instead of helping him."

But almost at once she realised that she had made a false step.

Sarah's face hardened. She moved to the dressing-table and took and lighted a cigarette. Then she said, lightly:

"You're quite the devil's advocate, aren't you, Mother?"

"What do you mean?"

Ann was bewildered.

Sarah came back and stood squarely in front of her mother. Her face was suspicious and hard.

"What's the real reason you don't want me to go off with Gerry, Mother?"

"I've told you—"

"The *real* reason. . . ." Very deliberately, her eyes boring into Ann's, Sarah said: "You're afraid, aren't you, *that I might be happy with Gerry?*"

"I'm afraid you might be very *un*happy!"

"No, you're not." Sarah shot the words out bitterly. "You wouldn't care if I was unhappy. It's my happiness you don't want. You don't like me. It's more than that. For some reason or other you hate me. . . . That's it, isn't it? You hate me. You hate me like hell!"

"Sarah, are you mad?"

"No, I'm not mad. I'm getting at the truth at last. You've hated me for a long time—for years. *Why?*"

"It's not true . . ."

"It *is* true. But why? It's not that you're jealous of me because I'm young. Some mothers are like that with their daughters, but not you. You were always sweet to me. . . . Why do you hate me, Mother? I've got to know!"

"I don't hate you!"

Sarah cried: "Oh, do stop telling lies! Come out into the open. What have I ever done to make you hate me? I've always adored you. I've always tried to be nice to you—and do things for you."

Ann turned on her. She spoke bitterly and with significance in her voice.

"You speak," she said, "as though the sacrifices had been all on your side!"

Sarah stared at her bewildered.

"Sacrifices? What sacrifices?"

Ann's voice trembled. She pressed her hands together.

"I've given up my life for you—given up everything I cared for—and you don't even remember it!"

Still bewildered, Sarah said: "I don't even know what you're talking about."

"No, you don't. You didn't even remember Richard Cauldfield's name. *'Richard Cauldfield?'* you said. *'Who's he?'*"

A dawning comprehension showed in Sarah's eyes. A faint dismay rose in her.

"Richard Cauldfield?"

"Yes, Richard Cauldfield." Ann was openly accusing now. "*You* disliked him. But *I* loved him! I cared for him very much. I wanted to marry him. But because of you I had to give him up."

"Mother . . ."

Sarah was appalled.

Ann said defiantly: "I'd a right to my happiness."

"I didn't know—you really cared," Sarah stammered.

"You didn't want to know. You shut your eyes to it. You did everything you could to stop the marriage. That's true, isn't it?"

"Yes, it's true . . ." Sarah's mind went back over the past. She felt just a little sick as she remembered her glib childish assurance. "I—I didn't think he'd make you happy. . . ."

"What right had you to think for another person?" Ann demanded fiercely.

Gerry had said that to her. Gerry had been worried by what she had been trying to do. And she had been so pleased with herself, so triumphant in her victory over the hated "Cauliflower." Such crude childish jealousy it had been—she saw that now! And because of it, her mother had suffered, had changed little by little into this nervy unhappy woman now confronting her with a reproach to which she had no answer.

She could only say, in an uncertain whisper:

"I didn't know . . . Oh, Mother, I didn't know. . . ."

Ann was back again in the past.

"We could have been happy together," she said. "He was

a lonely man. His first wife had died with the baby, and it
had been a great shock and grief to him. He had faults, I
know, he was inclined to be pompous and to lay down the
law—the sort of things young people notice—but underneath it he was kind and simple and good. We would have
grown old together and been happy. And instead I hurt him
badly—I sent him away. Sent him to a hotel on the south
coast where he met that silly little harpy who doesn't even
care for him."

Sarah drew away. Each word had hurt her. Yet she rallied to say what she could in her defence.

"If you wanted to marry him so much," she said, "you
should have gone ahead and done it."

Ann turned on her sharply.

"Don't you remember the eternal scenes—the rows? You
were like cat and dog together, you two. You provoked him
deliberately. It was part of your plan."

(Yes, it *had* been part of her plan. . . .)

"I couldn't stand it, going on day after day. And then I
was faced with an alternative. I had to choose—Richard put
it like that—to choose between him and you. You were my
daughter, my own flesh and blood. I chose you."

"And ever since then," said Sarah clear-sightedly, "you've
hated me. . . ."

The pattern was completely clear to her now.

She gathered up her furs and turned away towards the
door.

"Well," she said. "We know where we are now."

Her voice was hard and clear. From contemplating the
ruin of Ann's life, she had turned to the contemplation of
the ruin of her own.

In the doorway she turned and spoke to the woman with
the ravaged face who had not denied that last accusation.

"*You* hate *me* for spoiling your life, Mother," she said.
"Well, I hate *you* for spoiling mine!"

Ann said sharply: "I've had nothing to do with your life.
You made your own choice."

"Oh, no, I didn't. Don't be a damned hypocrite, Mother.
I came to you wanting you to help me not to marry Law-

rence. You knew quite well that I was attracted by him, but that I wanted to get free of that attraction. You were quite clever about it. You knew just what to do and say."

"Nonsense. Why should I want you to marry Lawrence?"

"I think—because you knew I wouldn't be happy. *You* were unhappy—and you wanted me to be, too. Come now, Mother, spill the beans. Haven't you had a certain kick out of knowing that I'm miserable in my married life?"

In a sudden flash of passion Ann said:

"Sometimes, yes, I've felt that it served you right!"

Mother and daughter stared at each other implacably. Then Sarah laughed, a harsh unpleasant laugh.

"So now we've got it! Good-bye Mother *dear*. . . ."

She went out of the door and along the passage. Ann heard the flat door close with a sharp sound of finality.

She was alone.

Trembling still, she reached her bed and flung herself down on it. Tears welled up in her eyes and flowed down her cheeks.

Presently she was shaken by a tempest of weeping such as she had not known for years.

She wept and she wept . . .

How long she had been crying she did not know, but as her sobs at last began to die down, there was a chink of china and Edith entered with a tea-tray. She put it down on the table by the bed and sat down by her mistress, patting her shoulder gently.

"There, there, my lamb, my pretty. . . . Here's a nice cup of tea and you're going to drink it down whatever you say."

"Oh, Edith, Edith . . ." Ann clung to her faithful servant and friend.

"There, there, don't you take on so. It will be all right."

"The things I said—the things I said—"

"Never you mind. Sit up now. I'll pour out your tea. Now you drink it."

Obediently Ann sat up and sipped the hot tea.

"There now, you'll feel better in a minute."

"Sarah—how could I—?"

"Now don't you worry—"

"How could I say those things to her?"

"Better to say them than to think them, if you ask me," said Edith. "It's the things that you think and don't say that turn bitter as bile in you—and that's a fact."

"I was so cruel—so cruel—"

"I'd say that what has been wrong with you for a long time was bottling things up. Have a good row and get it over, that's what I say, instead of keeping it all to yourself and pretending there's nothing there. We've all got bad thoughts, but we don't always like to admit it."

"Have I really been hating Sarah? My little Sarah—how funny and sweet she used to be. And I've hated her?"

"Of course you haven't," said Edith robustly.

"But I have. I wanted her to suffer—to be hurt—like I was hurt."

"Now don't you go fancying a lot of nonsense. You're devoted to Miss Sarah, and always have been."

Ann said:

"All this time—all this time—running underneath in a dark current—hate . . . hate . . ."

"Pity you didn't set to and have it out sooner. A good row always clears the air."

Ann lay back weakly on her pillows.

"But I don't hate her now," she said wonderingly. "It's all gone—yes, all gone. . . ."

Edith got up and patted Ann on the shoulder.

"Don't you fret, my pretty. Everything's all right."

Ann shook her head.

"No, never again. We both said things that neither of us can ever forget."

"Don't you believe it. Hard words break no bones, and that's a true saying."

Ann said:

"There are some things, fundamental things, that can *never* be forgotten."

Edith picked up the tray.

"Never's a big word," she said.

Chapter four

Sarah, when she arrived home, went to the big room at the back of the house which Lawrence called his studio.

He was there, unpacking a statuette that he had recently purchased—the work of a young French artist.

"What do you think of it, Sarah? Beautiful, isn't it?"

His fingers sensitively caressed the lines of the nude twisted body.

Sarah shivered a little, as though at some memory.

She said, frowning:

"Yes, beautiful—but obscene!"

"Oh, come now—how surprising that there is still that touch of the Puritan in you, Sarah. Interesting that it should persist."

"That figure *is* obscene."

"Slightly decadent, perhaps. . . . But very clever. And highly imaginative—Paul takes hashish, of course—that probably accounts for the spirit of the thing."

He put it down and turned to Sarah.

"You are looking very much *en beauté*—my charming wife—and you are upset over something. Distress always suits you."

Sarah said: "I've just had a terrific row with Mother."

"Indeed?" Lawrence raised his eyebrows in some amusement. "How very unlikely! I can hardly imagine it. The gentle Ann."

"She wasn't so gentle today! I was rather horrible to her, I admit."

"Domestic disputes are very uninteresting, Sarah. Don't let's talk about them."

"I wasn't going to. Mother and I are all washed up—that's what it amounts to. No, I want to talk to you about something else. I think I'm—leaving you, Lawrence."

Steene showed no particular reaction. He raised his eyebrows and murmured:

"I think, you know, that would be rather unwise on your part."

"You make that sound like a threat."

"Oh, no—just a gentle warning. And why are you leaving me, Sarah? Wives of mine have done it before but you can hardly have their reasons. I have not, for instance, broken your heart. You have very little heart where I am concerned and you are still—"

"The reigning favourite?" said Sarah.

"If you like to put it in that oriental manner. Yes, Sarah, I find you quite perfect—even the Puritan touch gives a spice to our—what shall I say—rather pagan mode of life? By the way, my first wife's reason for leaving me cannot apply either. Moral disapprobation could hardly be your strong suit, all things considered."

"Does it matter why I'm leaving you? Don't pretend that you'll really mind!"

"I shall mind very much! You are, at the moment, my most prized possession—better than all these."

He waved a hand round the studio.

"I meant—you don't *love* me?"

"Romantic devotion, as I once told you, has never appealed to me—to give or to receive."

"The plain truth is—there's someone else," said Sarah. "I'm going away with him."

"Ah! leaving your sins behind you?"

"Do you mean—"

"I wonder whether that will be as easy as you think. You've been an apt disciple. Sarah—the tide of life runs strongly in you—can you give up these sensations—these pleasures—these adventures of the senses? Think of that evening at the Mariana . . . remember Charcot and his Diversions. . . . These things, Sarah, are not to be so lightly laid aside."

Sarah looked at him, and for a moment fear peeped out of her eyes.

"I know . . . I know . . . but one *can* give it all up!"

"Can one? You're rather deep in, Sarah. . . ."

"But I shall get out . . . I mean to get out. . . ."

Turning she went hurriedly out of the room.

Lawrence put down the statuette with a bang.

He was seriously annoyed. He was not yet tired of Sarah. He doubted that he would ever tire of her—a creature of temperament, capable of resistance—of struggle, a creature of enchanting beauty. A Collector's Piece of extreme rarity.

Chapter five

"Why, Sarah," Dame Laura looked up from her desk in surprise.

Sarah was breathless and in a state of considerable emotion.

Laura Whitstable said:

"I haven't seen you for ages, god-daughter."

"No, I know . . . Oh, Laura, I'm in such a *mess*."

"Sit down." Laura Whitstable drew her gently to a couch. "Now then, tell me all about it."

"I thought perhaps you could help me. . . . Can one, does one—is it possible to stop taking things—when, I mean —when you've got used to taking them."

She added hastily:

"Oh, dear, I don't suppose you even know what I'm talking about."

"Oh, yes, I do. You mean dope?"

"Yes." Sarah felt an enormous relief at the matter-of-fact way in which Laura Whitstable reacted.

"Well, now, the answer depends on a lot of things. It's not easy—it's never easy. Women find it harder to break a habit of that kind than men do. It depends very much on how long you have been taking the stuff, how dependent you have got on it, how good your general health is, how much courage and resolution and will-power you have got, under what conditions you are going to pass your daily life, what you have to look forward to, and, if you are a woman, if you have someone at hand to *help* you in the fight."

Sarah's face brightened.

"Good. I think—I really think it will be all right then."

"Too much time on your hands isn't going to help," Laura warned her.

Sarah laughed.

"I shall have very little time on my hands! I shall be working like mad every minute of the day. I shall have someone to—to get tough with me and make me toe the line, and as for looking forward—I've got everything to look forward to—*everything!*"

"Well, Sarah, I think you've got a good chance." Laura looked at her—and added unexpectedly: "You seem to have grown up at last."

"Yes. I've been rather a long time about it . . . I realise that. I called Gerry weak, but *I'm* really the weak one. Always wanting to be bolstered up."

Sarah's face clouded over.

"Laura—I've been simply horrible to Mother. I only found out today that she'd really minded about Cauliflower. I know now that when you were warning me about sacrifices and burnt offerings I just wouldn't listen. I was so horribly pleased with myself, with my plan for getting rid of poor old Richard—and all the time I can see now I was just being jealous and childish and spiteful. I made Mother give him up; and then naturally she hated me only she never said so, but things just seemed to go all wrong. Today we had a terrific set to—and shouted at each other, and I said the most beastly things to her, and blamed her for everything that had happened to me. Really, all the time, I was feeling awful about *her*."

"I see."

"And now—" Sarah looked miserable—"I don't know *what* to do. If only I could make up to her in some way—but I suppose it's too late."

Laura Whitstable rose briskly to her feet.

"There is no greater waste of time," she said didactically, "than saying the right thing to the wrong person. . . ."

Chapter six

1

With rather the air of someone who handles dynamite, Edith picked up the telephone receiver. She took a deep breath and dialled a number. When she heard the ringing at the other end, she turned her head uneasily over her shoulder. It was all right. She was alone in the flat. The brisk professional voice coming over the wire made her jump.

"Welbeck 97438."

"Oh—is that Dame Laura Whitstable?"

"Speaking."

Edith swallowed twice, nervously.

"It's Edith, ma'am. Mrs. Prentice's Edith."

"Good evening, Edith."

Edith swallowed again. She said obscurely: "Nasty things, telephones."

"Yes, I quite understand. You wanted to speak to me about something?"

"It's about Mrs. Prentice, ma'am. I'm worried about her, I really am."

"But you've been worried about her for a long time, haven't you, Edith?"

"This is different, ma'am. It's quite different. She's lost her appetite, and she sits about doing nothing. And often I'll find her crying. She's calmer, if you take my meaning, none of that restlessness she used to have. And she don't take me up sharp any more. She's gentle and considerate like she used to be—but she's just got no heart in her—no *spirit* any more. It's dreadful, ma'am, really it's dreadful."

The telephone said "Interesting," in a detached professional manner, which was not at all what Edith wanted.

"It would make your heart bleed, really it would, ma'am."

"Don't use such ridiculous terms, Edith. Hearts don't bleed unless they have received physical damage."

Edith pressed on.

"It's to do with Miss Sarah, ma'am. Proper dust-up they had, and now Miss Sarah's not been nigh the place for nearly a month."

"No, she's been away from London—in the country."

"I wrote to her."

"No letters have been forwarded to her."

Edith brightened a little.

"Ah, well, then, Once she's back in London——"

Dame Laura cut her short.

"I'm afraid, Edith, you'd better prepare yourself for a shock. Miss Sarah is going away with Mr. Gerald Lloyd to Canada."

Edith made a noise like a disapproving soda-water siphon.

"That's downright wicked. Leaving her husband!"

"Don't be sanctimonious, Edith. Who are you to judge other people's conduct? She'll have a hard life of it out there —none of the luxuries she's been accustomed to."

Edith sighed: "That does seem to make it a little less sinful . . . And if you'll excuse me saying so, ma'am, Mr. Steene always *has* given me the creeps. The sort of gentleman you could fancy has sold his soul to the devil."

In a dry voice Dame Laura said:

"Allowing for the inevitable difference in our phraseology, I'm inclined to agree with you."

"Won't Miss Sarah come and say good-bye?"

"It seems not."

Edith said indignantly: "I call that downright hard-hearted of her."

"You don't understand in the least."

"I understand how a daughter ought to behave to a mother. I'd never have believed it of Miss Sarah! Can't you do something about it, ma'am?"

"I never interfere."

Edith drew a deep breath.

"Well, you'll excuse me—I know you're a very famous lady and very clever, and I'm only a servant—but this is a time that I think you ought to!"

And Edith slammed down the receiver with a grim face.

2

Edith had spoken twice to Ann before the latter roused herself and answered.

"What did you say, Edith?"

"I said as how your hair was looking peculiar round the roots. You ought to do a bit more touching-up of it."

"I shan't bother any more. It will look better grey."

"You'll look more respectable, I agree. But it will look funny if it's half-and-half."

"It doesn't matter."

Nothing mattered. What could matter in the dull procession of day that followed day? Ann thought, as she had thought again and again, "Sarah will never forgive me. And she's quite right . . ."

The telephone rang and Ann got up and went to it. She said: "Hullo?" in a listless voice, then started a little as Dame Laura's incisive voice spoke at the other end.

"Ann?"

"Yes."

"I dislike interfering in other people's lives, but—I think that there is something you perhaps ought to know. Sarah and Gerald Lloyd are leaving by the eight o'clock plane for Canada this evening."

"What?" Ann gasped. "I—I haven't seen Sarah for weeks."

"No. She has been in a nursing home in the country. She went there voluntarily to undergo a cure for drug-taking."

"Oh, Laura! Is she all right?"

"She's come through very well. You can probably appreciate that she suffered a good deal. . . . Yes, I'm proud of my god-daughter. She's got backbone."

"Oh, Laura." Words streamed from Ann. "Do you remember asking me if I knew Ann Prentice? I do now. I've ruined Sarah's life through resentment and spite. She'll never forgive me!"

"Rubbish. Nobody can really ruin another person's life. Don't be melodramatic and don't wallow."

"It's the truth. I know just what I am and what I did."

"That's all to the good then—but you've known it some time now, haven't you? Wouldn't it be as well to go on to the next thing?"

"You don't understand, Laura. I feel so conscience stricken—so horribly remorseful . . ."

"Listen, Ann, there are just two things that I've no use for whatever—someone telling me how noble they are and what moral reasons they have for the things they do, and the other is someone going on moaning about how wickedly they have behaved. Both statements may be true—recognise the truth of your actions, by all means, but having done so, *pass on*. You can't put the clock back and you can't usually undo what you've done. Continue living."

"Laura, what do you think I ought to do about Sarah?"

Laura Whitstable snorted.

"I may have interfered—but I haven't sunk so low as to give advice."

She rang off firmly.

Ann, moving as though in a dream, crossed the room to the sofa and sat there, staring into space. . . .

Sarah—Gerry—would it work out? Would her child, her dearly loved child, find happiness at last? Gerry was fundamentally weak—would the record of failure go on—would he let Sarah down—would Sarah be disillusioned—unhappy? If only Gerry were a different type of man. But Gerry was the man that Sarah loved.

Time passed. Ann still sat motionless.

It was nothing to do with her any longer. She had forfeited all claim. Between her and Sarah yawned an impassable gulf.

Edith looked in on her mistress once, then crept away again.

But presently the door-bell rang and she went to answer it.

"Mr. Mowbray's called for you, ma'am."

"What do you say?"

"Mr. Mowbray. Waiting downstairs."

Ann sprang up. Her eyes went to the clock. What had she been thinking about—to sit there, half paralysed?

Sarah was going away—tonight—to the other side of the world. . . .

Ann snatched up her fur cape and ran out of the flat.

"Basil." She spoke breathlessly. "Please—drive me to London Airport. As quick as you can."

"But Ann darling, what *is* all this about?"

"It's Sarah. She's going to Canada. I haven't seen her to say good-bye."

"But darling, haven't you left it rather *late?*"

"Of course I have. I've been a fool. But I hope it isn't *too* late. Oh, go on—Basil—quick!"

Basil Mowbray sighed, and started the engine.

"I always thought you were such a reasonable woman, Ann," he said reproachfully. "I really am thankful that I shall never be a parent. It seems to make people behave so oddly."

"You must drive *fast*, Basil."

Basil sighed.

Through the Kensington streets, avoiding the Hammersmith bottleneck by a series of intricate side streets, through Chiswick where traffic was heavy, out at last on the Great West Road, roaring along past tall factories and neon-lit buildings—then past rows of prim houses where people lived. Mothers and daughters, fathers and sons, husbands and wives. All with their problems and their quarrels and their reconciliations, "Just like me," thought Ann. She felt a sudden kinship, a sudden love and understanding for all the human race . . . She was not, could never be, lonely, for she lived in a world peopled with her own kind. . . .

3

At Heathrow the passengers stood and sat in the lounge, awaiting the summons to embark.

Gerry said to Sarah:

"Not regretting?"

She flashed a quick look of reassurance at him.

Sarah was thinner and her face bore the lines that the endurance of pain puts there. It was an older face, not less lovely, but now fully mature.

She was thinking: "Gerry wanted me to go and say good-bye to Mother. He doesn't understand. . . . If I could only make up to her for what I did—but I can't . . ."

She couldn't give back Richard Cauldfield. . . .

No, the thing she had done to her mother was beyond forgiveness.

She was glad to be with Gerry—going forward to a new life with him, but something in her cried forlornly. . . .

"I'm going *away*, Mother, I'm going *away*. . . ."

If only—

The raucous note of the announcer made her jump. "Will passengers travelling by Flight 00346 for Prestwick, Gander and Montreal please follow the green light to Customs and Immigration. . . ."

The passengers picked up their hand luggage and went towards the end door. Sarah followed Gerry, lagging a little behind.

"Sarah!"

Through the outer door Ann, her fur cape slipping from her shoulders, came running towards her daughter. Sarah ran back to meet her, dropping her small travelling bag.

"Mother!"

They hugged each other, then drew back to look.

All the things that Ann had thought of saying, had rehearsed saying, on the way down, died on her lips. There was no need of them. And Sarah, too, felt no need of speech. To have said "Forgive me, Mother," would have been meaningless.

And in that moment Sarah shed the last vestige of her childish dependence on Ann. She was a woman now who could stand on her own feet and make her own decisions.

With an odd instinct of reassurance Sarah said quickly: "I shall be all right, Mother."

And Gerry, beaming, said: "I'll look after her, Mrs. Prentice."

An Air official was approaching to herd Gerry and Sarah in the way they should go.

Sarah said in the same inadequate idiom:

"*You'll* be all right, *won't* you, Mother?"

And Ann answered:

"Yes, darling. I'll be quite all right. Good-bye—God bless you both."

Gerry and Sarah went through the door towards their new life and Ann went back to the car where Basil was waiting for her.

"These terrifying machines," said Basil, as an air-liner roared along the runway. "Just like enormous malignant *insects!* They frighten me to *death!*"

He drove out on to the road and turned in the direction of London.

Ann said: "If you don't mind, Basil, I won't come out tonight with you. I'd rather have a quiet evening at home."

"Very well, darling. I'll take you back there."

Ann had always thought of Basil Mowbray as "so amusing and so spiteful." She realised suddenly that he was also *kind*—a kind little man and rather a lonely one.

"Dear me," thought Ann—"What a ridiculous *fuss* I have been making."

Basil was saying anxiously:

"But Ann, darling, oughtn't you to have something to *eat?* There won't be anything ready at the flat."

Ann smiled and shook her head. A pleasant picture rose before her eyes.

"Don't worry," she said. "Edith will bring me scrambled eggs on a tray in front of the fire—yes—and a nice hot cup of tea, bless her!"

Edith gave her mistress a sharp look as she let her in, but all she said was:

"Now you go and sit by the fire."

"I'll just get out of these silly clothes, and put on something comfortable."

"You'd better have that blue flannel dressing-gown you gave me four years ago. Much cosier than that silly neglijay affair as you call it. I haven't ever worn it. It's been put away in my bottom drawer. Took a fancy to be buried in it, I did."

Lying on the sofa in the drawing-room, the blue dressing-gown tucked snugly round her, Ann stared into the fire.

Presently Edith came in with the tray and arranged it on a low table by her mistress's side.

"I'll brush your hair for you later," she said.

Ann smiled up at her.

"You're treating me like a little girl to-night, Edith. Why?"

Edith grunted.

"That's what you always look like to me."

"Edith—" Ann looked up at her and said with a slight effort: "Edith—I saw Sarah. It's—all right."

"Of course it's all right! Always was! I told you so!"

For a moment she stood looking down at her mistress, her grim old face soft and kind.

Then she went out of the room.

"This wonderful peace . . ." Ann thought. Words remembered from long ago came back to her.

"The peace of God which passeth all understanding. . . ."